The Complete FREDDY THE PIG Series
Available or Coming Soon from The Overlook Press

The Clockwork Twin

THE
CLOCKWORK TWIN

•

By Walter R. Brooks

WITH ILLUSTRATIONS BY
Kurt Wiese

THE OVERLOOK PRESS
Woodstock & New York

If you enjoyed this book, very likely you will be interested not only in the other Freddy books published in this series, but also in joining the *Friends of Freddy,* an organization of Freddy devotees.

We will be pleased to hear from any reader about our "Freddy" publishing program. You can easily contact us by logging on the either THE OVERLOOK PRESS website, or the Freddy website.

The website addresses are as follows:
THE OVERLOOK PRESS:
www.overlookpress.com

FREDDY:
www.friendsoffreddy.org

We look forward to hearing from you soon.

First published in the United States in 2003 by
The Overlook Press, Peter Mayer Publishers, Inc.
Woodstock & New York

WOODSTOCK:
One Overlook Drive
Woodstock, NY 12498
www.overlookpress.com
[for individual orders, bulk and special sales, contact our Woodstock office]

NEW YORK:
141 Wooster Street
New York, NY 10012

Dust jacket and endpaper artwork courtesy of the Lee Secrest collection and archive.

Cataloging-in-Publication Data is available from the Library of Congress

Brooks, Walter R., 1886-1958.
The Clockwork Twin / Walter R. Brooks ; illustrated by Kurt Wiese.
p. cm.

Manufactured in the United States of America
ISBN 1-58567-358-7
1 3 5 7 9 8 6 4 2

For Bernice Baumgarten

CONTENTS

The Clockwork Twin

1 The Voyage of the Summerhouse

Once there was a boy about your age, and his name was Adoniram R. Smith. When anybody asked him what the R stood for, he would say: "Oh, it's a silly name and I don't like it," and he would never tell. But when anybody asked him how he pronounced his first name, he would say: "Pronounce it to rhyme with 'Uncle Hiram.'" And I guess that is the best way to tell anybody how to pronounce it.

He lived in a farmhouse beside a big river

with his uncle and aunt, and they were not very nice to him. As soon as he came home from school they made him work until supper time, and when supper was over he had to go right to bed. In the summer when there wasn't any school, they made him work all day. They acted mad at him all the time, and what seemed to make them maddest was his name. When they wanted him to do anything they would call: "Adoniram! Adoniram!" and it is a pretty long name to call if you do it a hundred times a day. Still, they could have called him Ad or Don, or just "Here, boy!" But they weren't very bright, and so they never thought of that.

The river was deep and swift, and at night when it was very still you could hear it chuckling quietly to itself as it hurried by. But in the spring the chuckle grew to an angry roar, and the river rose higher in its banks and sometimes overflowed them, and snatched and tore at hen-coops and gates and woodpiles and carried them down with it. And one spring it rose so high that it came into the cellar of the house, and Adoniram could see barns and porches and parts of bridges whirling by on tossing brown water.

One night they were sitting at supper. It was a warm night, and the windows were open, and the rush and rumble of the river were so loud that they had to shout to make themselves heard. "Pass the butter!" Adoniram's uncle would bellow; and "Take your elbows off the table!" his aunt would shriek. They seemed just about as cross as usual, so he didn't think they were worried, although the river was rising.

"Adoniram!" his uncle roared suddenly.

"Yes, sir," shouted Adoniram.

"Go out and see if the river is any higher," bawled his uncle.

So Adoniram left the rest of his supper and went out to look at the stake that his uncle had driven into the ground at the edge of the water to measure its rise.

The grass that sloped down to the river was covered with swift-sliding, muddy water, and the little summerhouse on the edge of the bank, which in ordinary times stood eight feet above the water, was now a little island. Adoniram looked at it, standing up black against the afterglow, and hoped the river wouldn't carry it away. And he was just about to turn to look at the stake when he heard a sharp yelp and saw something small and dark scrabbling and splashing in the water and clinging to the summerhouse railing. And then a little voice called: "Help! Help!"

Adoniram hesitated, but only for a second, though he knew he would get a licking if he didn't go straight back into the house and report. Then he tore off his shoes and stockings and waded out. The water tugged at his legs, but it was only knee-deep, and he ran up the summerhouse steps, leaned over, and, grabbing a handful of wet fur, pulled a little brown dog up to safety.

The dog shook himself, sneezed, wagged a two-inch tail, barked twice, and sat down and looked at Adoniram. I don't know what kind of a dog he was. He had two ears, four legs, a tail, and a nose that was cold when he was well and hot when he had eaten something that disagreed with him. Just a dog.

"Well, doggy," said Adoniram.

The dog got up, barked, wagged his tail, and sat down again.

"Oh, dear," said Adoniram. "I thought you

could talk. I was sure I heard you call 'Help!' Didn't you, really?"

The dog scratched his ear, looked doubtfully at the boy for a minute, then said: "Yes. Yes, I did. But don't tell anybody."

"Oh, I won't tell," said Adoniram. "But look, doggy—"

"Georgie's the name," said the dog.

"Oh," said Adoniram. "Well, look, Georgie. I've got to go right straight back into the house, and I can't take you with me because they'd drive you away. But I'll take you over to dry land, and then—well, couldn't you stay around for a few days? In the barn, maybe, where they wouldn't see you? I'd bring you out bones and things—"

"Sure, sure," said Georgie. "A bone, or an old bread crust, or any odds and ends of leftovers—anything but bananas, in fact—"

"Don't you like bananas?"

"I'll tell you about that another time. But right now I think we ought to be getting out of here, don't you? If this summerhouse goes—"

"Oh, we're all right," said Adoniram. "The water'll have to get a lot higher and stronger to carry this away. But I've got to get back anyway." He picked up the dog under his arm and was just feeling under water for the top of the first step, when out of the corner of his eye he saw something huge and black and shapeless bearing down upon them.

"Look out!" yelped Georgie, and Adoniram had just time to hook an arm tight around a doorpost when the thing, looming as high as a house, swept down and seemed to swallow them. There was a creaking and cracking, twigs whipped across the boy's face, and the summerhouse rocked, and then with a splitting crash pulled loose from its foundations and was whirled off down the river in the branches of a big pine tree.

Luckily the summerhouse was wedged tight into the crotch of the tree trunk or it would have tipped over. But after swaying a few times as the trunk bumped along the bank, it swung out into the middle of the stream, and then it sped along down as smoothly and swiftly as a little steamboat. The needles were all about them. After a minute, when he had got over his scare, Adoniram put the dog down and peered out.

"Oh, dear," he said. "We've come a mile already. I'll catch it when I get home."

"I guess you don't need to worry about that for a while," said Georgie.

"No, I suppose not," said the boy. "This river gets wider and wider for hundreds of miles. Oh, Georgie, do you suppose we'll be carried right out into the ocean? And we haven't got anything to eat, either."

"Oh, what do you worry for?" said Georgie. "Why don't you enjoy the ride?"

"Enjoy it?" asked Adoniram doubtfully. He wasn't used to enjoying things, perhaps because he had never had much to enjoy. "Well, maybe you enjoy it, but I certainly don't. I wish I was back home."

Georgie sniffed and said: "Oh, well, go on and worry, then. But don't spoil my fun." And he went and sat on the other side of the summerhouse. But in a minute he came back again.

"Look here, boy," he said, "we hadn't ought to quarrel. Specially as you look so much like the boy that owned me. I suppose you haven't got a brother named Byram R. Jones, have you?"

"No," said the boy. "Adoniram R. Smith is

my name. I wish I did have a brother."

"What's the R stand for?"

"I won't ever tell anybody that," said Adoniram. "It's a silly name."

"Byram wouldn't tell what his R stood for either," said Georgie. "That's funny, isn't it? You both have a middle name you don't like, and you look just alike. Oh dear, I wish I could get back to Byram. I don't know how he'll get along without me."

"Where did you live?" Adoniram asked.

"In the city. A long way up the river. Byram didn't have any folks. Except me, that is."

"He didn't have any folks?" exclaimed Adoniram. "Well, but how did you get anything to eat, or a place to sleep, or—"

"He used to live with some people named Jones," said the dog, "and I guess he took their name. He didn't know what his real last name was, he said. But they weren't good to him, so he ran away. We lived in an old shed down by the railroad. We used to go out on the street together, and I'd turn somersaults and beg and play dead dog—just silly things like that—and then I'd pass his cap, and people would throw money into it. We made enough to buy things to eat, though once all we had for a week was bananas." Georgie shuddered. "I wouldn't peel another banana if I were starving to death!

"Then this flood came, and our shed was washed away. We were all right until just as we came round the bend above your house. I slipped and fell in. I didn't dare bark, because Byram would have jumped in after me, and probably we'd both have been drowned. So I swam hard and just managed to get to your summerhouse. Now we're separated, and I don't suppose I'll ever see him again. Byram was an awful smart boy."

It was getting lighter now, for the moon had come out from behind a cloud, and it turned the tumbling water to silver. Georgie looked out through an opening in the foliage and watched the lights along the shore swing by and sniffed the cool damp air, and every now and then he called Adoniram's attention to something. Pretty soon the boy sat down beside him.

"Isn't this fun?" said Georgie.

"Why—yes," said Adoniram. "Only I can't help thinking about—"

"About all the awful things that may happen —is that it?" asked the dog. "Well, why don't you think about how maybe they won't happen? Why don't you think about *nice* things that may happen? It doesn't cost any more. Maybe we *will* be carried out to sea. But then, maybe we'll be rescued by a warship or an ocean liner, and live on it, and maybe you'll learn how to run it, and maybe when you grow up you'll be captain."

"Oh, could I?" asked Adoniram.

"How do I know?" said Georgie. "But one thing's certain: there are hundreds of boys your age that are going to be sea captains some day and don't know it. Maybe you're one of them."

Adoniram had never thought about things that way before. But as soon as he began to think about them that way, he began to have a good time. And he and Georgie pretended they were on a ship, and he was captain and Georgie was mate. "Full steam ahead, mate!" he would shout, and Georgie would reply: "Aye, aye, sir!" Then Georgie would call: "Submarine off the port bow, sir!" and perhaps a floating barn would loom up close to them and they would pretend to fire shells at it. And once when they were pretending to shell a shed that was bobbing along beside them, the little building struck a log and flew to pieces as if it really had been struck by a shell, and they shouted and cheered like anything.

They had been doing this for about an hour when Georgie shouted: "Village off the starboard bow, sir!" Hundreds of lights twinkled on the hillside above the river, and at the edge of the water some motor-boats were pulled up and a lot of men were working under a floodlight. They shouted and barked, but though out where they were the roar of the water did not seem very loud, the men on shore could not hear them, and the summerhouse was so hidden in the leaves that they could not be seen. And they swept on by and pretty soon the lights grew dim in the distance.

Adoniram was surprised to find that he didn't much care, really. After all, if they were rescued, he would just have to go back to his uncle and aunt. "This *is* fun, Georgie," he said.

"Look," said the dog. "What's that?"

A small object was coming up behind them, and on top of it was something that moved.

"Ahoy!" shouted Georgie. "What ship is that?"

He was answered by a feeble crow.

"A rooster!" said Adoniram. "Stand by, mate. We'll rescue him."

He caught hold of the rail and leaned far out, but before the hencoop caught up he could see that he wasn't going to be able to reach it. Then he thought of something and, climbing on the rail, reached up under the roof and hauled down a small coil of fishline with a sinker at one end. There was no hook on it, because his uncle always took the hook off and put it in his hatband so Adoniram couldn't fish with it. But it was just what Adoniram wanted.

"Stand by to catch a line!" he shouted, and threw the sinker. The first throw missed, but the second time the sinker caught the rooster in the side, and with a terrified squawk he fell into the river. But he had the presence of mind to grab the line with his beak, and a minute later he was dragged into the summerhouse.

He ruffled his dripping feathers, shook them, settled them, and said peevishly: "I say, you might have aimed a little more accurately. You nearly sprained my wing."

"Say, listen," said Georgie, "we rescued you from a watery grave and is that what we get for it? Just complaints? Captain, what do you say we heave him back in?"

"Sorry," said the rooster; "say no more about it. I dare say you would be annoyed if you'd ridden seventy miles on top of that coop, and whirling around all the time so sometimes you were so dizzy you could hardly hang on. And I've got a cold, too, and that water won't help it."

He cleared his throat and tried to crow, but only a faint miserable piping came out that sent Georgie into a fit of laughter. Even Adoniram, who had never really laughed heartily in his life, had to smile.

"I say, you fellows," said the rooster indignantly, "this is a bit thick. Not very sporting, what?—to laugh at a fellow because he has a cold."

"I'd give an inch off my tail if I could make a noise like that, rooster," said Georgie. "Oh, don't get sore; we're all in the same boat. Ho, that's a good one, isn't it?—all in the same boat."

"What's funny about that?" said the rooster. "We *are* in the same boat, aren't we?"

"Sure. That's what I mean," said Georgie.

"Indeed!" said the rooster; "so we're in the same boat. And it's funny. Well, really!"

Adoniram had got out his handkerchief, and now he rubbed the rooster down and got most of the water off him, and then he tucked him under his coat to keep him warm. And pretty soon the rooster went to sleep.

"We'd better get a little sleep ourselves," said Georgie. "You might tie that line around us, captain, so we won't fall overboard in the night."

So Adoniram looped the line a few times around his waist and then through the dog's collar, and fastened it to the railing. Then they lay down on the floor close together. It was warm, and the rush and roar of the water was pleasant and drowsy. Adoniram listened for a while, and watched for a while the black and silver pattern of the moonlit pine boughs, and then he turned over on the other side without disturbing his companions and went to sleep.

II *The Shipwreck*

One very bad thing about being a rooster is
that you have to get up at sunrise and crow to
get the other chickens up. Most roosters don't
realize that the other chickens would get up anyway, and they feel that their job is a pretty important one. So when the rescued rooster poked
his head out from under Adoniram's coat and
saw the eastern sky all pink and misty, instead
of pulling it back again and taking another nap,
as he wanted to, he said: "Oh, my word! I must
arouse these sluggards!" And he crawled hastily
out and shook himself and hopped up on the

summerhouse rail and took a deep breath and—

Well, you could hardly say that he crowed. If *Cock-a-doodle-doo* is the way to write what a regular rooster does when he crows, what this rooster did can only be written as *Beep-a-weepy-weep*. It was just a thin little trembling pipe. He certainly had a terrible cold.

But the sound was so queer that it woke Adoniram and Georgie as quickly as if it had been a good loud crow. They sat up, looked around, and then Georgie began to laugh and after a minute Adoniram joined in. They laughed for several minutes while the rooster looked cross. But Adoniram, who didn't know how to laugh properly, got to coughing. So then the rooster began to laugh, and he went on for some time until Georgie said:

"Oh, keep still, rooster."

"I shall not be silent," said the rooster huffily, "unless you compel me to by force."

"Oh, I can stop you all right," said the dog. "Where do you expect to get breakfast? There isn't anything to eat on this boat, you know."

"What!" said the rooster, staring at him. "Nothing to eat? You mean to say you've lured me on to this—this structure only in order to starve me to death? You've rescued me, and now you refuse to offer me nourishment? Why, I never heard of such a thing."

"Yes, you have," said Georgie with a grin. "You just heard of it now."

"We're sorry," said Adoniram. "But we haven't got anything to eat either."

"Oh, my word," said the rooster. "Oh, upon my soul!" And he walked away from them to the other side of the summerhouse and stood gloomily peering out through the pine needles at the tossing river, which under the red sunrise looked like a river of red paint.

"Well, I stopped his laughing all right," said Georgie, "but I stopped my own, too."

"What are we going to do?" asked the boy. "I'm pretty hungry. I only had part of my supper last night. And I'm thirsty, too."

"Mustn't drink the river water," said Georgie. "It'll make us sick. Oh well, cheer up. I expect we'll be rescued before long. We've come a long way in the night and I've heard that there are some big towns down the river. There are sure to be some boats out looking for people."

"But they can't hear us, and they can't see us in all these pine needles."

"Suppose you break away some branches and try to make a couple of windows in the tree," said Georgie, "and then you can wave your handkerchief. They'll see that."

So Adoniram got to work, and pretty soon the rooster came back and apologized for being so unpleasant, and helped. Of course he couldn't break off branches, but he climbed out on the limbs and picked off sprays that Adoniram couldn't reach. And in a little while they had two good windows, one on each side.

The river had grown much wider in the night. Even now that it was broad daylight, they could sometimes hardly make out the shore line. Most of the time they were held to the middle of the river by the current, but once in a while it would swing them in toward one bank or the other, and then they could see trees and telephone poles rising from the flood, and even the roofs of submerged barns and houses. Once it swung them in very close to a hill on which stood a farm. Several cows were standing on the shore, looking with mild surprise at the angry, tossing water. Adoniram waved to them, but Georgie gave a frightened whimper and crowded close to him.

"What's the matter?" the boy asked.

"Oh, those—those awful creatures! Why, I've seen big dogs before, but never any like that, with horns!"

"Why, those are nothing but cows," said Adoniram.

"Well, I don't care what you call 'em. I just hope there aren't many of them in this part of the country, that's all."

"You mean to say you've never seen a cow before?" asked the boy. "Why, every farm in the country has some. That's where the milk comes from. There are thousands and thousands of them."

"Oh dear," said Georgie, "I wish I was back in the city. I always thought the country was nice and safe and peaceful, but if there are a lot of those great, ferocious, horned things around, I guess I'm a gone pup."

So Adoniram explained about cows, and by and by Georgie felt better.

To take their minds off their empty stomachs,

Adoniram asked the rooster if he wouldn't tell them the story of his life. The rooster, whose name was Ronald, was more than willing, like most roosters, to talk about himself, but the story of his life, although he gave it everything he had, didn't take very long in the telling. It explained one thing, though. That was the funny way he talked. For he was English. He had been sent over to this country as an egg, and had been hatched out on a farm up-river that raised fancy poultry. He had indeed taken several prizes at poultry shows.

"Well, if you came over as an egg," said Georgie, "I don't quite see why you have such a strong English accent."

"My dear chap!" said Ronald. "After all, I *am* English, even if I did come over inside a shell and never saw England. And this English accent is useful at the shows. One could hardly win prizes as an English rooster if one hadn't an English accent. Of course," he said, dropping the accent all at once, "I was brought up with American chickens, and I can talk American as well as you guys. You're darn tootin', I can. How about it, buddy, isn't that somethin'?"

"Sure, that's American you're talking now," said Georgie. "Oh, look; there are some boats."

But they had moved out again into the middle of the river, too far from the boats to be noticed.

As the morning went on they grew hungrier and hungrier and thirstier and thirstier. And then at last the river carried them swiftly round a long curve and they saw before them the closely pressed houses and high towers of a city.

Almost before they had time to realize it they were surrounded by buildings. But the muddy water was lapping at the second-story windows and it was plain that the buildings were empty. Not a face showed at any window, and, perhaps because the water ran so swiftly, no boats were in sight. The water here, too, was troubled by cross-currents, and the tree whirled and jerked and occasionally bumped heavily, so that the summerhouse swayed and shook and they had to hold on to the railing to keep from being thrown overboard.

As they got farther into the city the cross-currents got worse. Once an eddy at the corner of a big factory building set them whirling like a merry-go-round for five minutes, and when, released from that, they shot again downstream, a side current caught them and carried them out of the main stream of the river entirely and down a wide street. Here they moved more slowly. It was evidently one of the main shopping streets, for they passed a hotel, and the water splashed muddily against the signs over the doors of shops and stores. And then the tree trunk stopped with a jerk, wedged between a lamp-post and a wall, and the branches swung around and came close up against a large building on which was a big sign: Waterman Dinkelstein & Co.

The summerhouse was shoved tight up against a window, and Adoniram reached out and tried to open it, but it was locked.

"We'll have to smash it in," said Georgie.

So Adoniram swung the fishline with the sinker on the end against the window until the glass broke, and then he reached in and undid the fastening. A minute later boy and dog and rooster were standing in a huge room through which ran several rows of pillars. And between the pillars were lines of show-cases. They were in the men's furnishings department of a big department store.

Adoniram had never been in a city before. The biggest store he had ever seen was the general store at Snare Forks, near his uncle's house. "My goodness," he exclaimed, staring at a showcase full of neckties, "I didn't suppose there were so many neckties in the world!"

"We can't eat neckties," said Georgie. "Come on, captain. Let's find some food."

So they left the men's furnishings and went through the shoes and the overcoats and the rugs and the musical instruments, and up a flight of stairs and through the ready-made dresses and the lamps and the underwear and the stationery. They found a drinking fountain, but no water came out of it.

"I hope the groceries aren't on the ground floor," said Georgie, "or we're sunk. Ha ha, not bad, eh? Sunk, and so are the groceries!"

They went on through the electrical appliances and the refrigerators and the picture framing and the curtains and up another stairway and through a door and there in front of them was a long counter, and on it was every kind of pie and cake and bun and cookie that you can imagine.

26

Georgie grabbed a doughnut, and the rooster fluttered up and perched on the edge of a tray of seed rolls, and Adoniram picked up a crisp brown cinnamon bun. They all took a bite and three chews, and then at the same moment they stopped. They were too thirsty.

If it hadn't been for Georgie I don't know what would have happened to them, for Adoniram didn't know anything about department stores, and the rooster wasn't any help. But Georgie said the one word: "Bottles!" and hurried off, and after looking at each other a minute, the other two followed. They passed shelves and shelves of canned things and breakfast foods and crackers and jams and jellies and at last Georgie gave a sharp bark and stopped in front of a sort of bin full of bottles of ginger ale. Luckily there was an opener behind the counter. So they opened three or four bottles and drank. And then they opened some bottles of cream soda and drank that. And then they weren't thirsty any more.

But the sad part of it was that they had drunk so much that when they went back to the buns and pies and cakes they couldn't eat any of them.

They were hungry still, but they just didn't have the room.

"You might have stopped me!" said the rooster, gazing angrily at the seed rolls. "Let me drink all that slosh! If I was turned inside out, I could swim. I heard a distinct splash when I jumped up on this counter."

"Oh, stop complaining about everything," said Georgie good-naturedly, "or you'll hear a distincter splash when we throw you back into the river. The ginger ale will settle down after a while and then we can eat. In the meanwhile let's explore."

"Won't the store people be mad if we eat up all this food?" Adoniram asked as they started up to the fifth floor.

"You couldn't eat it up in ten years," said the dog, "and we're shipwrecked sailors anyway. I guess they wouldn't— Psst!" he whispered suddenly. "What's that?"

They had come out at the head of the stairs on to another huge floor on which stood thousands of chairs and tables and desks and dressers and beds. Nobody was in sight, but from somewhere came a voice. It seemed to be reciting poetry. The voice said:

"When I set out upon this tour,
I thought the skies would be much bluer."

There was a pause and then it went on:

"When I set out upon this tramp,
How could I know 'twould be so damp?

When I set out on this excursion,
I did not think it meant submersion.

When I set out upon this trip
I should have started in a ship."

There was a pause again, and another voice —a quicker and sharper voice—said: "Swell, Freddy. Keep it up. You've got twelve now."

"Oh, it's nothing; I could keep it up for hours," said the other voice modestly. At least the tone was modest, but Adoniram didn't think the words were, very. "When I set out upon this—"

"*A—a-a-chew!*" went the rooster, who had been standing in a draught.

Two heads suddenly appeared above the back of the largest and softest davenport in the room.

2 9

One was large and pinkish white and rather pleasing in expression, and that was a pig. And the other was smaller and black, with yellow eyes and rather elegant whiskers, and that was a cat. Both looked startled.

The cat spoke first. "Hi, folks," he said breezily. "Well, where'd you come from?"

"Hello," said Adoniram, and the dog said: "We came down the river. My name's Georgie, and this is Adoniram, and—"

"Adoniram!" said the cat. "Go on!"

"Yes, it is," said the boy. "That's my name."

"Really?" said the cat. "How do you pronounce it?"

"Oh, don't be funny, Jinx," said the pig. "Adoniram—that's a good name. But very hard to find a rhyme to. Well, welcome to Waterman Dinkelstein & Co. This is Jinx, and I am Freddy. I think I didn't catch the name of your friend?"

The rooster ruffled his feathers and stepped forward importantly. "My name is Ronald," he said. "You may have heard of me, gentlemen?"

"Possibly," said Jinx, the cat, indifferently.

"I don't want to make a point of it," said the

rooster, "but I am well known at all the best poultry shows, and have indeed several times won prizes."

"Ah," said Jinx. "A prize rooster, eh? Well, I don't follow the poultry shows much. I dare say you'd taste the same to me as any little scrub chicken." And he winked at Adoniram.

"Come along," said Freddy, the pig, to Ronald, who had begun to back away from the cat, "sit down and join the party. Jinx doesn't mean anything. How did you get here?"

So they sat down and told their story. When they had finished, Freddy said: "I guess we were all pretty lucky to have taken refuge in a place where there is plenty to eat. Jinx and I are rather enjoying it, but of course we're in no special hurry to get home. We're on our vacation. That is, partly business and partly vacation.

"You see," he went on, "we live on a farm back in New York State. We're kept pretty busy there most of the time, and so when work slacks off, a few of us always go away for a little trip. One winter a lot of us even went to Florida. Of course we arrange it so our work is taken care of

31

while we're away. Jinx, for instance, gets a skunk friend of his to look after the mice in his absence. My own work is of a special nature, but my partner, Mrs. Wiggins, looks after it."

"You will pardon me," said Ronald, who had been silent a long time for a rooster, "but I had never supposed that there was anything special about what pigs do on a farm."

Jinx gave a snort. "That shows how little you know about pigs, rooster. Freddy here is a poet, he's an inventor, he's the best detective in Otesaraga County, he's a pig in the best sense of the word, a pig with two g's. Of course we know what you mean. You mean that pigs are supposed to do nothing but eat. Well, what is there to be ashamed of in that? You eat, don't you? So do I. Sometimes I eat roosters, and what do you know about that?" And he grinned at Ronald, who shrank away from him with drooping tail-feathers.

But Freddy said: "There, there, Jinx. I'm sure Ronald didn't mean anything." And, turning to the rooster: "Don't let Jinx scare you. He's rough and noisy, but he's the tenderest-hearted cat that ever lived. Why, I've seen him shed tears over a little chicken that had lost its mother. Yes, sir, genuine tears, rolling right down his whiskers. Why—"

"Oh, lay off me, will you, Freddy?" said Jinx, looking embarrassed. "Go on with your story."

"Well," said the pig, "as I was saying, we take these trips every year. But one thing has bothered us. We collect things—you know, little souvenirs of our travels, picture postcards and so on—but it's hard to bring them home. There isn't any way to carry them. Boys, now, have pockets. But animals have to carry everything in their mouths. So it occurred to me— why not pockets for animals?"

"Say, that's a good idea!" exclaimed Georgie.

"And it works," said Freddy. "Get one for him, Jinx. I think we've got his size."

Jinx looked at the dog. "Take about a six, I should say," he said. Then he jumped down from the davenport and went over to a chair where he rummaged among what seemed to be a pile of rags, then came back with a strange-looking object which he worked over Georgie's head. When he had straightened it out, they could see that it had two large pockets, woven of string and grass like birds' nests, which hung down on each side like saddlebags, and a sort of collar that held it in place.

"Fits as if it was made for him," said Jinx. "Here, take a look, dog." And the cat led him over to a mirror, near the elevator, where Georgie stood for several minutes admiring himself, speechless with pleasure.

Presently he came back and started to take the pockets off again, but Freddy said: "No, no. Keep it on. It's yours if you want it."

"But don't you sell them?" said Georgie.

"No. We may work out some way of selling them later, but at present we're just introducing the idea. That's what I meant when I said we were taking this trip partly as vacation and partly on business. We got some of the birds to make up a couple dozen pockets of assorted sizes, and we started out with them to see how the public received them. I must say every animal we've tried them on seems delighted with them. Freddy's Fitz-U Animal Pockets, we call them. All styles, all sizes. Patent pending."

"What does that mean?" asked Georgie.

"We don't know," said the pig. "But you

have to have it on them. Then, as I was saying, we got caught in this flood. We stopped at a deserted farm a few miles above the city three days ago, and when we got up in the morning the water had surrounded us. We rode down here on a barn door and got in just as you did. —But aren't you fellows hungry?"

"I guess I could eat something now," said Adoniram, and Georgie and Ronald said they could too.

"Come on, then," said Freddy, getting up. "Let's go down to the grocery department. I'm glad you're here, Adoniram. There are a lot of things in cans we wanted to try, but we couldn't get into them. Plum pudding, for one thing. Boy, I don't care if the water doesn't go down for six months!"

III *Escape from Snare Forks*

There are lots worse places to be shipwrecked in than a department store. For three days the water stayed at the same level, then it began to drop slowly, an inch or so every hour. But the animals were in no hurry to get away, and neither was Adoniram. He had a grand time. At home he had never had any fun, or anything very good to eat, and he had never had any time to play with the other children he went to school with. But now, with these animals who laughed and talked and played games and told stories all day long, he was really happy. The first time he laughed out loud Freddy looked at him sharply and said:

"We'll have to oil up that laugh of yours, Adoniram. I guess you haven't used it much. It squeaks like an old rusty hinge."

So twice a day Freddy would give him laughing lessons. The pig would sit down and tell jokes until Adoniram laughed good and hard, and then he would laugh with him for as long as they could keep it up. At first it took four or five pretty good jokes to get the boy started. But after a day or two his laugh began to get loosened up, and finally when he laughed ten minutes at a rather poor joke Freddy said he guessed that was enough.

"You don't want to be one of these people who laugh too much," said the pig.

They lived most of the time in the furniture department. They moved the furniture around so that each one of them had a room with a bed and a table and a radio and two or three big comfortable chairs and anything else he wanted. Freddy had a desk in his, and from the stationery department he brought all sorts of paper and envelopes and pencils and blank books to make notes in and a typewriter. He could use the typewriter, too, unlike most pigs. He used to sit there a good deal, tapping out poetry, and letters to the friends at home. Of course they were never mailed, but, as Freddy said, that didn't matter, because most of his friends couldn't read anyway. Jinx's room was, as you would expect, full of squashy soft cushions, and he had a cupboard full of mechanical mice that he used to wind up and chase for exercise. They fixed up rooms for the newcomers, and in Adoniram's was a wonderful table that opened up and was full of all kinds of games.

They had put a bed in Ronald's room, and although roosters usually sleep on a perch, he thought that because of his cold he had better sleep in the bed, where he could be covered up. But it didn't work very well because he couldn't seem to manage the pillow, which kept falling down on top of him and nearly smothering him. So he gave it up and perched on the footboard.

Every evening they had a banquet. They would go down about six o'clock to the grocery department and look along the shelves, picking out the things they wanted for dinner. Then

Adoniram would open all the cans and boxes and jars and they would spread them out on a long counter and start in. Sometimes there were as many as eighteen courses. Of course they all ate too much, but animals have more sense than humans about eating, and Adoniram was the only one that got sick. That was on the first day, and you can't really blame him for eating until his eyes bulged. Most anybody would do the same. After that he took Freddy's advice and ate more sensibly.

It was a pretty pleasant life. There were all sorts of games, and they even gave a play, in costumes from the children's wear department. Freddy wrote it for them. It was a detective play and he said it was based on some actual experiences of his own. Of course he added quite a lot to these, because besides detectives and burglars and watchmen he had a lot of historical characters in it—Roman soldiers and President Hoover and Lafayette and Napoleon. That made it confused, but lots of fun. Ronald quite blossomed out on the stage, too. He was splendid as Napoleon.

But the most fun for Adoniram was exploring

the store. He found the toy department, where there were hundreds of games, and aeroplanes that would fly, and construction sets, and an electric train with switches and signal lights and yards and yards of track. And he found the sporting goods department, crammed with guns and fishing tackle and bicycles and tents and camping outfits and practically everything you can use outdoors. And when he got tired of these, he could go down to the book department, and there were thousands of brand-new story books full of pictures. And he could always run down to the bakery for a pocketful of cookies or a slice of cake. Probably it was just as well for him that the candy department was on the ground floor, under six feet of water.

On the ninth morning they heard noises in the street, and the sound of men shouting. They looked out and saw that the water was gone, and through the deep gray mud that covered everything half a dozen men in hip boots were clumping along.

"Time to go, boys," said Freddy. "They'll be opening for business in a day or two now, and they won't want us around. We'll start in an hour. And now the question is: you three have lost your homes, so why don't you go home with us?"

"Sure," said Jinx. "Mr. Bean can always use an extra dog and an extra rooster around the place. And he'd like to have you, too, Adoniram. You see, Mr. and Mrs. Bean haven't any children of their own, although they always wanted some. A few years ago they adopted a boy and girl that we rescued from a terrible place up in the North Woods. But now Ella and Everett have gone abroad for a year with Mrs. Bean's sister, and the Beans are alone again. We've been hoping we could find somebody to take their place, but most children wouldn't want to leave their families, even if their families would let them. But from what you've said, I don't expect you want to go back home much, do you?"

"No," said Adoniram, "I don't. But—well, they're my uncle and aunt. Maybe they're worried. Maybe they're looking for me. I—I guess I ought to go back."

"Well, you know best about that," said Freddy. "We won't try to persuade you. But if you change your mind, there's always a home for you on the Bean farm. Come on, now. Get your stuff together."

In less than an hour they were ready for the road. The animals had put on their pockets, which were bulging with supplies from the grocery department, and they had even fixed a pair of pockets for Ronald which he had loaded up with puffed rice and a couple of seed rolls. The garment was much too large for him; it hunched up over the shoulders and dragged on the ground, so that except for the tail-feathers sticking out behind, he looked like a very small boy wrapped up in a large shawl.

Adoniram had thought that he oughtn't to take anything but food with him, but Freddy said that he was sure the store people wouldn't mind if he outfitted himself with things that he really needed for the trip. So he wore rubber boots and a slicker and carried on his back a knapsack in which he had packed plenty of food, a change of clothing, and a few things he might need if he camped out—matches, a scout knife, a mess kit, and so on.

"A regular swamp!" exclaimed Freddy as they

came carefully down the slimy stairs to the ground floor, which was inches deep in gray mud. "Hop on my back, Ronald. And, Adoniram put Jinx on your shoulder. They can never get through this."

Indeed, it was almost impossible for the boy and the pig to get through. The mud sucked at their feet and hampered them so that they were ten minutes getting to the door. Outside, however, it was not so bad. The water was still running off, cutting little rivulets through the slime, and by walking in the flowing water they had easier going.

Freddy led the way, and at first they met no one, but they were going uphill all the time and pretty soon they got into a part of the city where the flood had not been so deep. Here men were busy repairing houses and washing down the streets with fire hose. But nobody paid much attention to them, and it wasn't until they got out into dry streets above flood level that they saw a rope stretched across the street in front of them, and several policemen on guard.

"Hey, boy!" shouted one of the policemen. "Come out of there!"

"Don't let 'em know we can talk," muttered Freddy as they went forward.

"Don't you know you aren't allowed inside the flood lines?" demanded the policeman. "Where'd you get those things? You know you can be put in jail for stealing inside the lines?"

"I didn't steal them," said Adoniram.

"That remains to be seen," said the policeman, taking out a notebook and a very small pencil. "In the meantime you'll answer a few questions. Name?"

"Adoniram R. Smith."

"Come again," said the policeman, licking the pencil.

So Adoniram spelled his name three times, and at last the man wrote it down. Only he spelled it "Annarodinam." And after he had licked the pencil again and made the capital A bigger and blacker he said: "What's the R stand for?"

"It's a silly name," said Adoniram. "I don't ever use it."

"All names are silly," said the policeman. "Come on; what is it?"

"I don't want to tell," said the boy.

44

"Refuses to give name," said the policeman, and wrote that down. "Residence?"

"Snare Forks."

"Snare Forks!" exclaimed the policeman. "Never heard of it. You know where it is, Mike? Ed? Elmer? Any of you?" And when all the other policemen shook their heads, he licked the pencil and wrote: "Gives false address."

While this was going on, the animals had edged closer and closer to the rope, and all at once Freddy yelled: "Come on, boy!" and dove between the policeman's legs, upsetting him into the street. The animals ran, and Adoniram tried to follow them, but the policeman named Elmer caught him by the tail of his slicker.

The first policeman scrambled to his feet. "Ha!" he exclaimed. "Resisting arrest, eh? Where's my pencil? Catch those animals, boys."

"Let 'em go, sarge," said Elmer. "They'll find their way back to their owners, I expect."

"But where's my pencil?" roared the sergeant. "What is the matter with you men? Here we catch a dangerous criminal with dozens of charges against him—pig-stealing, cat-stealing, dog - stealing, rooster - stealing, boots - stealing, slicker-stealing, and goodness knows what else, and what do you do? Stand around and gawp! You look like policemen, you're dressed up like policemen, you wear badges and carry sticks and take the city's pay, and there isn't one of you that can keep track of a little thing like a pencil. Bah! You—you make me ashamed of the force!"

"Excuse me," said Adoniram, "but I noticed you when you fell down, and I—I think you swallowed the pencil."

"What!" shouted the sergeant, turning pale, except for the black marks around his mouth where he had licked the pencil lead. He stared at the boy, then suddenly clutched his stomach. "Carry on, Elmer," he said, and bolted into the police station.

"Well now, Adoniram," said Elmer, "suppose you just tell us your story in your own way. Don't mind the sergeant. He's kind of impetuous, and great on rules, but his heart's in the right place."

"So's his pencil," said another policeman.

"That'll do, Mike," said Elmer sternly. "Now, boy."

So then Adoniram told his story, though he

didn't say much about the animals, and when he had finished, Elmer said: "Well, we'll have to find out where Snare Forks is and then try to get in touch with your folks and send you back home. In the meantime come into the station house and we'll fix you a cup of cocoa. We'll take care of you all right."

"But I didn't mean to steal anything, really I didn't," said Adoniram.

"I'm sure you didn't," said Elmer. "And, what's more, the sergeant is sure of it, too. But you see, he likes to scare people. He thinks people ought to be afraid of policemen, so they won't commit crimes. I don't agree with him there. I don't think scaring people does any good. But anyway, you haven't anything to worry about."

So Adoniram stayed in the police station for four days. He quite got to like the sergeant, who when he wasn't suspecting you, was as nice a person as you'd care to meet, and full of exciting stories about police work. But Adoniram missed the animals. They were the only real friends he had ever had. And when on the fifth day the sergeant told him that his uncle had been heard from, and that he was to be sent home on the train, he came very near crying, for he felt sure that he would never see Freddy and Jinx and Georgie and Ronald again.

Adoniram changed at Winthrop to a bus which took him to Snare Forks. But from there he had to walk the three miles home, because his uncle said he couldn't spare the time to meet him. And when he got home and had told his story, he got scolded for two hours and spanked for five minutes—which is much too long for anybody to be spanked, even a hardened criminal—and then his uncle said that since he didn't seem to care much for his home, but preferred to go wandering about the countryside, he would have to give up the room he had always had and sleep in the barn. So his uncle gave him a blanket and another short spanking to remember the first one by and sent him out to the barn.

The barn was really much nicer than the house. The hay was soft and sweet-smelling, and the moonlight came in through the wide doorway and splashed everything with mysterious silver light. The policemen had allowed

Adoniram to keep the things he had taken from Waterman Dinkelstein & Co., and although his uncle had taken most of them away from him, he still had the scout knife and the mess kit. He kept them under a board in the barn floor, and at night he could take them out and polish them and play with them. But his uncle forced him to work harder than ever now, to make up for the time he had lost, and so he didn't get much time to play.

Every morning when he got up he washed his face at the pump in the barn. It wasn't easy to do, because his uncle wouldn't give him a basin to wash in, so he had to pump with one hand and wash with the other. His aunt wouldn't give him a towel, either, because she said he'd only get it dirty. So he had to dry off by going out and waving his arms around in the early morning sunshine. And he was doing this one morning after he had been home about a week, and wishing he was back in Waterman Dinkelstein & Co.'s furniture department with his friends, when away up over the hill behind the house he heard a rooster crow.

Now, there was nothing unusual about this,

for roosters were crowing all over the country-side that morning. But if you have made any study of roosters, you will know that no two of them crow exactly alike. And there was a funny squeak in the middle of this rooster's crow that was exactly like Ronald's. For although Ronald's cold had gone, it had left him with a very weak crow. Adoniram stopped waving his arms and listened, and in a minute the rooster crowed again.

"Oh dear," said Adoniram, "I wish that *was* Ronald. Only of course it can't be. But still, I wonder what a rooster is doing up there. There's nothing but woods over the hill." And so instead of going to the house to do the work he had to do before breakfast, he climbed up across the fields to the top of the hill.

At first he didn't see anything but more fields sloping down toward the deep woods. And then on a stone wall about half-way down, something fluttered, and the rooster crowed three times, and at the same time in the grass in front of the wall he could just make out some animals moving about. "It *is* Ronald!" Adoniram shouted, and galloped down the hill.

The animals came forward to meet him. "Well, well," said Freddy, "what a time we've had finding you! All we knew was that you lived near Snare Forks, so we've been visiting every farm along the river, and poor Ronald has nearly worn his crow out. We were sure you'd recognize it, but it's a good thing we found you today, because he couldn't have lasted much longer."

"I should say not," said Ronald. "You haven't a cough drop about you, have you, old chap? My throat is raw."

"Oh, I'm glad you came!" Adoniram exclaimed. "I didn't think I'd ever see you again."

"It's harder to get rid of friends than it is to make them," said Jinx. "And we couldn't just run off that way and leave you. We were pretty sure they'd send you home."

"And what we really came for," said Georgie, "was to see if you wouldn't change your mind and come with us."

"Yes," said Adoniram, "I will. My aunt and uncle don't like me, and I don't see why I should have to stay with them."

"Hurray!" said Jinx. "Well, let's get going."

"I can't go yet," said the boy. "My uncle

would miss me, and he'd catch us and bring me back. And anyway, there are some things I want to take with me."

So the animals agreed to wait in the woods the rest of the day. And then when Adoniram came out to the barn to go to bed, they would meet him and start.

Everything went smoothly. Adoniram got spanked again for being late for breakfast, but he managed to smuggle his knapsack and some clothing out of the house, and he got his scout knife and mess kit from under the barn floor and packed everything up. And at eight o'clock that night when he came down to the barn, the animals were waiting.

"We won't waste any time," said Freddy. "We'll have to travel all night, because we want to be a long way from Snare Forks by daylight. Come on."

So the travelers, each with his pack on his back, filed out of the barnyard and up over the hill. Jinx led the way, because cats can see better in the dark than other animals. They cut down behind the woods and struck into a road, and then as they trudged along, Freddy struck

up the old marching song that he had made up
when the animals took their first trip to Florida.

> Oh, it's over the hill and down the road
> And we'll borrow the moon for a light,
> And wherever we go, one thing we know:
> The road will lead us right.
>
> If you start from home by any road,
> And follow each dip and bend,
> What fortune you find, whether cold
>   or kind,
> You find home again at the end.
>
> Oh, the roads run east, and the roads
>   run west,
> And it's lots of fun to roam
> When you know that whichever road
>   you take—
> That road will lead you home.

IV Mr. Bean's Farm

"The nice thing about taking a trip," said Freddy, "is that it is just as exciting to come back home as it is to start out."

It was the twelfth morning since they had left Snare Forks, and they were standing on a hill looking down on a little valley, and on the side of a hill across the valley was a small white farmhouse and a big red barn and a lot of other buildings, all very neat and shining in the bright sunlight. And that was Mr. Bean's farm.

They sat down and rested for a few minutes,

and Jinx pointed out the houses where the different animals lived. "That big building with the blue curtains is the cow-barn," he said. "Mrs. Wiggins, Freddy's partner in the detective business, and her two sisters, Mrs. Wurzburger and Mrs. Wogus, live there. And that little house with the chimney is the henhouse, where you'll live, Ronald. Mr. Bean put in steam heat last year, and mahogany perches. I tell you, he spares no expense where his animals are concerned."

"I'm pretty dirty," said Adoniram. "Couldn't we wash somewhere before we see the Beans?"

So they went down and washed in the brook at the foot of the hill, and Adoniram took clean clothes out of his knapsack and put them on. And then they started for the farm.

There was nobody in sight as they came in the gate, but when they were half-way across the barnyard the little blue curtains at one of the windows of the cow-barn were pushed aside and a big white face appeared.

"Hi, Mrs. Wiggins!" called Freddy.

"Mercy on us!" exclaimed the cow. "It's Freddy and Jinx." And she came rushing out to greet them, and Mrs. Wogus and Mrs. Wurz-burger came after her.

Now, when Mrs. Wiggins said anything, you could hear her across two fields and a pasture. And when she raised her voice, you could hear her in the next county. So in two minutes the barnyard was full of a mob of cows and dogs and horses and chickens, all pressing around the travelers and shouting and laughing and slapping them on the back. Ronald was quite terrified by the racket, and Georgie, though his tail kept wagging, pressed close against Adoniram.

The animals all asked questions at once. "How did the pockets go, Freddy?" "Where'd you get the boy?" "Been eating any crows lately, Jinx?"

But suddenly the noise quieted down, and a small man in overalls with bushy gray whiskers came shoving through the crowd. He carried a pitchfork with which he made threatening gestures, but Adoniram noticed that he was careful not to touch any of the animals with it. "Quiet!" he shouted. "Tarnation, animals, can't ye stop this rumpus? Ye make more noise 'n a hop-pickers' picnic."

"It's Mr. Bean," said Freddy to his guests.

The farmer pulled Jinx's whiskers and poked the pig in the side. "Glad to see ye back," he said gruffly. Mr. Bean was not a demonstrative man; he never gushed. "And who may these be?" he asked.

"My name is Adoniram R. Smith," said the boy, "and this is Georgie and this is Ronald. We thought—well, we'd like to live here if—if you'd like to have us."

"Glad to have you," said Mr. Bean. "And Mrs. B.'ll be gladder. Consider that settled." He scratched a match on the seat of his trousers and lit a small pipe that Adoniram hadn't noticed before because it was almost hidden by his whiskers. He puffed hard at it for a minute until his whiskers oozed smoke like a brush fire, and then he said: "You look hungry, boy. You'll find Mrs. B. in the kitchen. She'll fix you up. Freddy, you know where to put the other two where they'll be comfortable. And you other animals," he added, "I suppose you'll be havin' a celebration tonight. But lights out at ten o'clock, remember." And he turned and stumped away.

As Adoniram went toward the house, Mrs. Bean came to the door to shake the breakfast crumbs from the tablecloth. She was small and plump, and as neat as Mr. Bean was untidy. She pushed her spectacles up on her forehead and stared, and then she said: "Land sakes, if it isn't Freddy and Jinx!" And she ran out and hugged the cat and patted the pig and shook hands with Ronald and Georgie. Then she looked at Adoniram.

"Well, well," she said, "you're a nice-looking boy, I must say. Now isn't it lucky I baked a big batch of molasses cookies yesterday? Do you live around here?"

"No, ma'am. I came with Freddy and Jinx. I—I ran away from home."

"Ran away from home!" exclaimed Mrs. Bean. "Well, you come right in the house and have something to eat, and then you can tell me all about it."

While Adoniram was inside telling his story, the animals went back to their work, for when anyone returned from a trip he always gave a lecture on his travels that night in the big barn, and they knew they would hear all about it then.

Freddy and Jinx took Ronald down to the chicken house and introduced him to Charles, the rooster, and his wife, Henrietta, and saw that he was assigned to a perch. And they introduced Georgie to Jock, the collie, and saw that he was taken care of. And then they walked down to Freddy's study, to arrange their picture postcards and make some notes for their lecture that evening.

Freddy's study was a comfortable little room that he had fixed up in a corner of the pigpen. Here were all his books and papers, and his typewriter, and an old easy chair that he could sit in when he wanted to think, or take a nap, or both. They slipped off their pockets and piled them on the floor, and Jinx jumped up on the typewriter table, while Freddy threw himself into the chair, out of which a cloud of dust rose that set the cat sneezing.

"This place gets worse and worse," said Jinx. "You haven't house-cleaned since you moved in here, I bet."

"I know," said the pig, "but I don't want to do it myself, and I hate to get the squirrels to do it. Nosey little brutes, poking among my papers.

They'd mix everything up, and probably lose half of 'em—"

"No great loss, I should say," remarked Jinx, looking over a heap of magazines and clippings piled beside him. "H'm. Cross-word puzzles. Old *St. Nicholas* with half the leaves torn out. Recipe for pumpkin pie—what use is that to you, I'd like to know? . . . 'How to make your own lipstick at home'—ha ha! Freddy you slay me! . . And here's a piece about that mechanical man they had at the circus last year. 'Walks, talks, plays games.' With a plan of how he's put together. . . . And an 'Ode to Spring,' from the Centerboro *Guardian*. Listen to this, Freddy. This is rich!

> O spring, O spring,
> You wonderful thing
> O spring, O spring, O spring!
> O spring, O spring,
> When the birdies sing
> I feel like a king,
> O spring!

Six verses of it—golly, what stuff! And signed 'Shakespeare, Jr.' Can you beat that? Boy, how he fancies himself!—Why, what's the matter, Freddy?"

For Freddy had turned slightly red and was frowning at his friend. He didn't have a very good frown, because he was pretty fat, and when he drew his eyebrows down, they just closed his eyes and he looked as if he was asleep. But Jinx knew what it meant.

"Oh, I'm sorry, Freddy, if I've hurt your feelings. Did you—was this something *you* wrote?"

"It's the first poem I ever wrote," said Freddy stiffly. "Naturally, I don't think now it's a masterpiece, but it showed enough promise for the *Guardian* to print it. And as to the—" He broke off suddenly as a queer jangling of chimes and little bells drifted in through the open window. "What on earth—!"

The two animals dashed out. The sounds came from the big barn, but by the time they reached the door everything was quiet again. Inside they could see Hank, the old white horse, munching away peacefully at his hay.

"What's the row, Hank?" Jinx asked.

Hank turned his head. He looked a little like Mr. Bean with the hay sticking out of his mouth in all directions. Then his voice came through the hay, saying something that they couldn't understand.

"What?" said Jinx. "I wish you wouldn't talk with your mouth full."

Hank swallowed with an effort, coughed, and said: "Sorry, boys. What row you mean? I ain't heard any row."

"Who's upstairs?" asked Jinx, whose sharp ears had caught the sound of somebody moving about up in the loft.

"That?" said Hank. "Why, Uncle Ben, of course. Oh sure, I forgot. He came while you were away. He lives here now." And Hank turned to pull down another bite of hay from the rack.

"Hey, wait a minute," said Freddy. "If you begin chewing again we'll never get a thing out of you. Who is he? Where'd he come from?"

"Mr. Bean's uncle. He used to be a clock-maker, but he's retired now. Same as you retired, I guess, Freddy, because he keeps right on pulling clocks to pieces just like you keep on detectin'."

"What's he like?" asked Jinx.

"Like Mr. Bean, only more so. More whiskers, more not sayin' anything. Go on up. He likes animals, seems like. At least he never throws 'em out. They say he's smart as all get-out about machinery, though. I wouldn't know about that. Never had much use for machinery myself since I got my tail caught in that thrashin' machine that time. You can't trust it. Though I dunno—I guess it's useful, at that."

The two animals climbed the steep stairs and came out in the dimly lit loft. At the far end, by the big door through which the hay was hoisted in, was a long work-bench on which stood several clocks with their insides strewn about them, and on shelves and on the wall above, fifty clocks were ticking busily away. A little man who looked like a smaller and older and hairier Mr. Bean was working away at the bench.

He turned as the animals came in, nodded to them, and went back to his work. They sat and watched him for a minute, then got up and walked around, looking at the clocks. There were banjo clocks and cuckoo clocks and grandfather clocks and clocks that told the month and the year and when the sun rose and even the weather. Some had little figures that came out and danced when they struck the hour, and there was one that delighted Jinx, because it had three mice that came out and ran up over the top every quarter-hour and then back into a hole underneath as a cat's head poked out in the middle of the dial and grinned at them.

Uncle Ben didn't say anything, but he watched them, and by and by he got up and started some of the clocks striking so they could see how they worked. And when the clocks chimed or cuckooed or the little figures popped out and in again, he would wink at Freddy and pull Jinx's tail. So they knew he liked to have them there.

But after he had gone back to his work and they had watched him awhile, he took the clock he had been working on and wound it up and set it in the middle of the floor. Then he said: "Clear out now, animals. Danger."

So they went downstairs again.

"He told us to beat it," Jinx said to Hank. "I thought you said he never did that?"

Hank had finished his hay and was taking a

nap until Mr. Bean should come out to give him some more. His eyes were closed, but he opened them very quickly.

"Eh?" he said. "What? Ordered you out, did he? Thunder! I suppose he's going to shoot that thing off again. I do wish he wouldn't. Goodness knows I don't think I'm asking too much—just a little peace and quiet to—"

Bang! There was a loud explosion upstairs. Jinx gave a screech and leaped three feet in the air and Freddy tried to dive under the old phaeton that stood on the barn floor, but missed his aim and got his head stuck between two spokes of a front wheel. There was a patter and jingle of little pieces of metal falling to the floor upstairs, and a small brass clock-wheel bounced down the stairs.

"There, thank goodness," said Hank, swishing his tail nervously, "it's over for today. Until he gets a new one built tomorrow."

"Hey, what is all this?" asked Freddy. "Get me out of this, will you?" He jerked and shook at the wheel, but his head was stuck fast.

Hank backed out of his stall and walked over

and looked at the pig, and Jinx joined him.

"We've got him where we want him now, eh, Hank?" said the cat.

"Looks like he was going to stay there for a spell, anyway," said Hank.

"Oh, quit being funny!" said Freddy angrily. "Can't you *do* something? Catch hold of me and pull."

"We could if you weren't so fat," said Hank, "but there ain't anything for anybody to get hold of. There's your tail, of course, but I dunno. It ain't much of a tail, and if I was to give a good yank on it, I wouldn't say but it'd come off. Try it if you say so, though."

"No, no!" said the pig anxiously.

"I've got it," said Hank suddenly. He turned with his back to the wheel, lifted one of his iron-shod hind hoofs, glanced over his shoulder to aim, and then kicked hard against the rim. The wheel flew off of the wagon with a crack and it and the pig slid across the floor.

Freddy struggled to his feet with the wheel still around his neck. "Now you have done it!" he said crossly. "I'll never get it off now. There's nothing to push against."

"Well, I shouldn't mind," said Jinx with a grin. "Looks kind of nice that way. You look kind of like Queen Elizabeth, with a big ruff around her neck. Eh, Hank?"

"Maybe his head would slip through if you was to soap it," said the horse.

"That's an idea!" said Jinx. He dashed out of the barn and was back presently with a piece of soap. "Come over to the watering trough, Freddy. I couldn't get kitchen soap; Mrs. Bean was there. So I snuck upstairs and got some of her best soap out of the bathroom. It's perfumed, I guess. Do you mind?"

"I don't care *what* it is," said Freddy. "Get me out of this thing."

So Jinx went to work and shampooed the pig thoroughly. Freddy squealed and twisted, for a good deal of the soap got in his eyes and mouth. But when Jinx said: "O.K. Now pull," his head slipped out easily.

Freddy didn't dare open his eyes, so his friends led him down to the duck pond. Alice and Emma, the two ducks, who were swimming about like two white powder puffs in their little pond, began to quack nervously when they saw this strange animal with the body of a pig and a shape-less white head of soapsuds.

"It's all right, girls," shouted Jinx. "It's only the great detective in disguise."

"Good gracious!" said Alice. "How clever! I should never have known him."

"Nor should I, sister," said Emma. "Mercy, you'd never guess he was a pig. And he smells so nice. But what is he disguised as, Jinx?"

"A marshmallow," said the cat. "Put him in a candy box and tie him up with a pink ribbon, and you'd never know the difference."

"I guess you could tell when you bit into him," said Hank.

"Oh, come on, come *on!*" said Freddy angrily. "Get me into the water."

"You asked for it," said Jinx, and he led the pig to the edge and shoved him in.

You hardly ever find a pig who is an expert swimmer, but then you hardly ever find one who is a good detective. Freddy was both. He swam across the pond with a fine racing stroke, then came back under water and stuck his head up be-tween the two ducks, scaring them good. Then he climbed out and chased Jinx, who hated to get wet, twice around the pond <u>and up a tree</u>. And then he sat down and laughed good-naturedly.

"Come on down, Jinx," he said. "I won't shake water on you. I'm really much obliged to you. And I want to find out about that explosion."

So Jinx came down and they all three sat down on the bank, and Hank said:

"Well, you see Uncle Ben has invented a new kind of alarm clock. He says that the kind with bells aren't much good, because people get used to the bells after a while and don't wake up when they ring. I dunno. What folks want alarm clocks for anyway beats me. What's the use of getting up unless you have to?"

"Well, but they do have to get up," said Freddy. "That's why they set the alarms."

"So Uncle Ben says. But I never could see why. . . . Well, anyway, he's invented a clock that fires off a firecracker. That ought to get 'em up, he thinks. But the trouble is, when the firecracker goes off, it blows the clock all to pieces. So it isn't any good now except for rich folks who can afford to have a new clock every morning."

"Yes," said Freddy thoughtfully. "Yes. But

70

there ought to be some way of getting round it."

"What do you want to get round, Freddy?" said a deep voice, and they turned to see Mrs. Wiggins standing behind them. "My goodness," the cow went on, "first it's detecting and then it's pockets for animals. All this thinking! I don't believe it's healthy. What is it now?"

So Freddy explained.

"Well, good grief!" said Mrs. Wiggins, "if the firecracker blows the clock to pieces, don't put the firecracker in. That's just common sense."

"Yes," said Freddy, "but it's *part* of the clock. You have to put it in, or you haven't got an alarm clock that shoots off a firecracker."

Mrs. Wiggins looked puzzled. "You've got your argument wrong end to, Freddy. It's when you put it *in* that you haven't got the clock. My stars, if I want to shoot off a firecracker, I don't swallow it first! Not if I ever want to shoot another."

"Now don't *you* start shooting firecrackers," said Hank. "One around the place is enough. —Hey, Freddy, what's the matter?" For the pig, who had been looking thoughtfully at Mrs. Wiggins, suddenly leaped up, shouted: "I've got it!"

and dashed off toward the barn.

The others looked after him. "I expect he's got another idea," said the cow placidly.

"I dunno where he gets 'em all," said Hank. "In fact, I dunno as I know what an idea is. I never had any myself, I'm thankful to say. They look kind of unpleasant to me—make you run around and yell. Folks are better without them."

But Freddy's idea carried him up the barn stairs two at a time. On the stool in front of the work-bench was Uncle Ben, his elbows on his knees, his chin in his hands. Freddy could not see his expression because of the whiskers, but his eyes were shut and his forehead drawn together in a deep frown, denoting thought.

Freddy hesitated a minute, but Uncle Ben did not open his eyes, and the pig tiptoed over to the end of the bench on which lay the plan of the alarm clock that Uncle Ben had been working from. It was a perfectly clear plan. There was the outline of the clock and pictures of all the little wheels, and the wheel that went around when the alarm went off and struck a match that lighted the firecracker fuse. There was the firecracker, too, and Freddy could see where Uncle

Ben had erased it several times in order to put it in another place.

So Freddy picked up a pencil and erased the firecracker again, and then he drew a big firecracker *outside* the clock and drew a long fuse leading in to where the match was. Then he took the plan over to Uncle Ben and nudged him. And Uncle Ben opened his eyes.

Uncle Ben was a smart man all right. As soon as he saw the changes that Freddy had made in the plan, he realized that if he had the firecracker go off outside, the clock wouldn't be blown to pieces. He jumped up and grabbed Freddy and waltzed all around the loft with him and then he got his tools and went to work. He didn't say anything at all, but it is surprising how little you have to say to let people know you are pleased.

After a while Freddy went downstairs again. Going through the barnyard he passed Mrs. Wiggins. The cow lifted her big nose and sniffed appreciatively. "H'm," she said. "Roses!" And passed on.

Freddy looked after her suspiciously, then started for the pigpen. A group of chickens were standing by the corner of the barn. When they saw him they began to whisper and giggle and then started toward him. He tried not to notice them as they, too, began sniffling the air ostentatiously, but when one of them simpered: "Oh, how too, too delicious! Like a breath of Spring!" he turned and chased them, fluttering and squawking, back to the henhouse.

Then he sniffed himself. Undeniably there was still a faint odor of perfumed soap clinging to him. But he decided it wasn't worth the bother of taking another swim to try to get it off. Whether he smelt of it or not, he knew that it would be weeks before the joke would completely lose its savor for his friends. He shrugged his shoulders and went on.

v The Clockwork Boy

Mr. and Mrs. Bean had been pretty lonesome
after Ella and Everett, their adopted children,
had gone away. But after Adoniram came they
weren't lonesome anymore. Mrs. Bean was happy
because she had someone else to make pies for,
and someone to talk to when Mr. Bean was out
working or when he went to sleep after supper.
And Mr. Bean was happy because Mrs. Bean was
happy. Mrs. Bean went around singing a good
deal. She sang different words, but it was always

the same tune—if it is really a tune when it is all on the same note. But that doesn't mean that she wasn't just as happy as if she had had a fine soprano voice and had gone around singing grand opera.

"It's funny," said Mrs. Wiggins to her sisters, "but I kind of like to hear Mrs. Bean sing."

"I guess it doesn't matter what a noise sounds like," said Mrs. Wogus, "as long as you know that it means something nice." Mrs. Wogus was inclined to be philosophical. That is, she liked talking without thinking much what she was talking about. But sometimes she said pretty wise things.

Adoniram was happy too. He had lots of good things to eat, and a whole big farm to play on, and all kinds of animals to play with. He liked the Beans a lot, although he was a little afraid of Mr. Bean at first, until he found out that his gruffness was all on the outside, like the shell on a peanut. The laughing exercises had been stopped, for he could now laugh at a joke like anybody else. But Freddy was not entirely satisfied. "You can smile and grin and giggle and chuckle all right. And you can laugh in a gentlemanly sort of way, too.

But boys hadn't ought to laugh in a gentlemanly way when things tickle them. They ought to open their mouths and yell 'Ha ha!' good and loud. Like Mrs. Wiggins. I think you ought to study her laugh. Remember: he whose laugh lasts, laughs best. And there's another thing to remember. You're not a really good laugher until you know when to stop. If you laugh too long, it sounds foolish. Some laughers make it a rule to stop after the fourth or fifth 'Ha.' That doesn't work very well for me, because sometimes I want to stop sooner, and other times I can't stop so soon. I think the best rule is to laugh good and loud and then stop as soon as you can."

So Adoniram tried that.

There were only two things that worried Adoniram. Georgie had tried pretty hard to find some traces of Byram. He asked every animal he met, but nobody had seen such a boy. He appealed to Freddy, who as a detective knew how to go about finding anything that was lost, but Freddy couldn't get any word about him either, although he appealed to the birds, who, as anyone knows, see a lot more of what is going on in the world than animals do. Adoniram worried about that.

But he worried more about what his aunt and uncle might do. For after he had been at the Beans' for a few days, Mrs. Bean told him that she had written to them.

"You see, Adoniram," she said, "Mr. Bean and I like you and want to have you live with us. But the only way we can do that is to adopt you. If we don't adopt you, your aunt and uncle can come any time and take you away. We don't any of us want that. So Mr. Bean and I decided the best thing was to write them about it. Don't you worry; we're not going to give you up."

But Adoniram did worry. He knew his aunt and uncle, and he knew that they wouldn't give him up either. He knew that they wanted to keep him, because he had often heard them talking about what they would do when he grew up and got strong enough to do all the work on their farm. His uncle wanted to open a hot-dog stand, and his aunt wanted to take lessons on the piano. They had never had time to, when they had so much work to do.

But after a couple of weeks had gone by and no answer had come to Mr. Bean's letter, Adoniram began to stop worrying. After all, there were so many things to do on the farm that there was hardly time for it. For one thing, there was Ronald's marriage.

One day Charles, the rooster, stopped Adoniram in the barnyard. "Could you spare me a moment of your valuable time on a private matter of some importance?" he asked pompously.

"Of course," said the boy.

"Just step down behind the cow-barn for a moment," said Charles, and when they were there: "This chap, Ronald," he said; "can you tell me anything about him? Do you—are you acquainted with his family at all?"

"Why, no," said Adoniram. "You know I just fished him out of the river. I don't know where he came from. Except that he's English. He said he had won a lot of prizes at poultry shows. That's about all I know about him."

"Poultry shows," said Charles, shaking his head. "Dear, dear, I was afraid of something like that." He thought deeply for a moment. "I have nothing against him, you understand," he said, "but it seems to me that in one who aspires to become a part of my immediate family, a taste for the bright lights and senseless revelry of poultry shows is definitely detrimental. Definitely," he said after a pause.

And after a moment he added: "Pernicious influence."

"You mean he wants you to adopt him?" asked Adoniram.

"In a sense, yes," said Charles. "He has asked me for the claw of my eldest daughter, Cackletta, in marriage."

"Well, but poultry shows aren't so awful, are they?" asked the boy. "Of course I don't know much about them—"

"Ah, but I do, young man, I do," interrupted the rooster. "Not that there is anything really wrong about them. Settled and serious-minded persons like you and me would not be hurt by attending an occasional show. There is no harm in throwing aside responsibility and being gay and care-free for an evening. But if this Ronald is merely an idle and irresponsible fellow, a hanger-on at poultry shows, who cares about nothing but a good time, then I shall withhold my consent. For I do not care to entrust my little Cackletta to—"

"Charles!" interrupted a sharp voice. "Where

on earth— Oh, there you are!" And Henrietta, Charles's wife, came bustling round the corner. She said hello pleasantly enough to Adoniram, whom she liked, and then turned to her husband. "I've been hunting all over the farm for you," she said crossly. "I thought you were going down to see Freddy about getting out the invitations, and there's the wedding breakfast to arrange about, and I'm pretty nearly crazy with so many things to do and the wedding only two days off, and all you do is stand around and gab, gab, gab."

"All right, my dear, all right," said Charles. "I'm going."

"You bet you're going," snapped Henrietta. "And, Adoniram, I wish you'd go along with him to see he gets there; and see that *when* he gets there he tells Freddy about the invitations. Fine thing—wedding two days away and the invitations not out yet because he can't stop talking long enough to order them. If talk was worth ten cents an hour he'd be the richest rooster in the world."

Charles didn't wait to hear any more, although there always was plenty when Henrietta was around, and Adoniram thought, as he followed the rooster down to the pigpen, that if talk was money, Henrietta would probably be just about as rich as her husband.

"But is the wedding all decided on, then?" he asked.

"Well, yes; in a manner of speaking," said Charles. "Fact of the matter is, Henrietta was quite taken with Ronald at the first. Don't misunderstand me; I like him myself. And, after all, that's the important thing, isn't it? This poultry-show business—it can't have done him much harm. No, upon mature consideration, I do not think I shall withhold my consent."

By the time they found Freddy, Charles was himself again, and being himself, for Charles, was feeling as important as all the Presidents of the United States from Washington down. They ordered the invitations, however, and Freddy went to work at them at once.

The wedding, two days later, was really quite a magnificent affair. The henhouse was much too small to accommodate all the guests, so it was held in the big barn, which was tastefully festooned with pink crepe paper. All of Charles's and Henrietta's relatives on neighboring farms were there, and one young rooster, a third or fourth cousin, walked eight miles and was so tired when he got there that he couldn't be present at the ceremony but had to be put to bed. Quite a romance grew out of this, for he fell in love with the bride's sister, who took care of him the two days he had to stay in bed and rest, and two weeks later they, too, were married.

Of course all the farm animals came, and neighborhood friends, and some of the woods animals; and the barn was crowded to the doors. Adoniram was there too. After the ceremony, which was performed by Ferdinand, the crow, the animals all pushed forward to offer their congratulations.

"Aren't you going to kiss the bride?" asked Hank, who had been standing beside Adoniram. "Customary at weddings—always kiss the bride."

The idea of kissing a chicken seemed pretty funny to the boy, and he laughed. But Hank said: "Well, I'm going to. It's bad luck not to, my mother used to say."

Some of the other animals had heard what the horse said, and they began to laugh too, and pretty soon all the animals in the barn were laughing, and they made a lane for Hank so he could walk right up to the bridal party. Cackletta looked a little scared, but she was her mother's daughter and when Hank knelt down carefully and put his big nose forward, she stretched out her beak and gave him a peck.

Then a skunk named Sniffy Wilson, who lived back in the woods, said he guessed he'd like to kiss the bride too. But Sniffy was suspected of having eaten one of Cackletta's little sisters, who had gone into the woods to pick wintergreen berries one day and had never come back. So Henrietta said no, they had to draw the line somewhere. "If you've got to kiss somebody," she said, "why don't you kiss Hank?"

"Not if I know myself," said the horse, backing away.

"Silence, please, everybody," shouted Ferdinand in his hoarse voice. "We will now listen to a speech by the bride's father."

"Gosh, I'm leaving!" said Jinx, and began to edge toward the door. A number of other animals evidently had the same idea, and as Charles hopped up on to the dashboard of the old phaeton, the barn became suddenly less crowded.

"Ladies and gentlemen," began Charles, "friends and well-wishers, it is my pleasure and my privilege to come before you on this happy and auspicious occasion to say a few words in the name of the happy pair who have just been joined together in the bonds of matrimonial wedlock. It is a happy occasion, I say, and yet, my friends, it is a sad occasion too. For while Ronald, here, the gay and gentlemanly Ronald, hero of a score of poultry shows, has gained a lovely bride, I, I, Charles, who stand before you, have lost a cherished daughter. Yet, my friends, 'twas ever thus . . ."

"You bet 'twas ever thus when Charles gets a chance to sound off," said Jinx to Freddy, as they came out into the bright barnyard, where refreshments were being served. "A good deal more thusness than I can stand."

"There's one thing about Charles's speeches," said the pig. "Nobody has ever found out how they end."

"I expect the happy pair, as he calls 'em, will have to find out how this one ends," said Jinx. "Everybody else is leaving, but they'll think they ought to stay."

"Adoniram's staying, too. He's politer than we are, Jinx."

"He's a nice boy."

Freddy was silent for a minute. Then he said: "I've been thinking a lot about Adoniram lately. He's been having a pretty good time since he came here. All the animals like him and they're always ready to play with him, and Mrs. Bean can't do enough for him. But just the same, he ought to have another boy to play with."

"I expect he'll go to school in Centerboro next year," said the cat.

"Centerboro is too far away for him to have much fun playing with the boys he'll meet there. And there isn't a boy on any of the farms around here."

"You mean you think we ought to find another boy for the Beans to adopt?"

"They'd adopt one if we could find one, all right. But where are you going to find one? Most boys have families or something. No, I've got another idea. Come on down to my study. I've got something to show you."

So the two friends left the crowded barnyard, where the wedding guests were feasting and dancing and enjoying themselves. As they passed the barn door they peeked in. Charles, all unconscious that his only remaining listeners were the bride and groom and Adoniram, all three of them sound asleep, was still orating away like anything. "The fourteenth consideration which I wish to bring before this distinguished gathering," he shouted, "is respect due to parents. How often, my friends, we see children who—"

"I never can think of Charles as a parent, somehow," said Freddy, as they went on.

"More like a phonograph," said Freddy. "How do you suppose he remembers it all?"

"He doesn't. I think he just keeps going around and starts all over again every ten minutes. Nobody ever listens, so nobody has ever found him out."

When they got to his study, Freddy spread out a large piece of paper before Jinx. Neatly lettered at the top were the words: "Plans and Specifications for Playmate for Adoniram," and then there was a big drawing of a clockwork boy, with hundreds of little wheels and levers and springs and things, all very carefully drawn.

"You remember that plan of the mechanical

man you saw on my desk?" Freddy asked. "Well, I've been working on that for some time, anyway, because I was interested in it. And then I thought, if we couldn't get a real boy to play with Adoniram, maybe we could get Uncle Ben to build a clockwork one, and I took this chart up to him a few days ago, and he's started to work on it already. What do you think of it?"

"Well," said Jinx, "I'm like Hank: I don't know much about machinery. He looks terrible complicated. What can he do?"

"Run, walk, dance, wrestle, throw a ball—oh, lots of things. And Uncle Ben is thinking up some more improvements."

"He won't be able to talk, will he? What good's a playmate that can't talk?"

"No, but we're going to put a yell in him. Most boys yell more than they talk, specially when they're playing."

"H'm," said Jinx, "what happens when he runs down?"

"He goes to sleep until you wind him up again."

"H'm," said Jinx again; "I'd hate to have a playmate I had to wind up all the time."

"Say, look, Jinx," said Freddy a little crossly, "I didn't tell you about this so you could think up a lot of criticisms. You leave all those things to Uncle Ben. What I wanted you to do was paint the face. You're good with paints, got a real artistic touch. We've got the head all cut out of wood and ready, and I thought it would be a good time when all the other animals are stuffing themselves with wedding cake and won't be snooping around, to get it done."

"Lead me to it," said Jinx enthusiastically. Like all cats, and many people, he wasn't much interested in any kind of work or game that he wasn't good at. But he was really good at painting, and so he became all at once very much excited about the clockwork boy.

Late that night, when all the guests had gone and lights were out, one small candle still burned up in the barn loft, where Jinx was putting the finishing touches to the wooden face with a small brush. At last he threw down the brush and stood back, purring with satisfaction. "There," he said, "when better faces are painted, Jinx'll paint 'em." And indeed he had done a splendid job. The face was as lifelike as paint could make it, and it looked exactly like Adoniram, even to the three large freckles on the bridge of the nose.

"Wonderful!" said Jinx. "Oh boy, are you a clever cat!" Then he turned and poked Freddy, who had agreed to sit up with him while he worked, but had gone to sleep.

"Eh? What? Who is it?" exclaimed Freddy, struggling to a sitting position. "Oh, it's you, Jinx. Yes. Was just taking forty winks while you finished."

"Forty snorts is more like it," said the cat. "Well, look. How do you like it?"

"Gosh," said Freddy, "that's swell, Jinx. It's so much like Adoniram that—well, I don't believe we'll be able to tell 'em apart."

"I wish I'd had somebody besides Adoniram to paint from," said Jinx. "It may be a bother, having them look alike. But there wasn't any other boy around."

"I don't see what difference it makes," Freddy said.

So then they both stood silently admiring the face for a while. But Freddy was pretty sleepy, and at last he said: "Well, let's go to bed."

"You go along," said Jinx. "I want to—well,

there's one or two little things—"

Freddy grinned. He knew that Jinx just wanted to admire his own work a little longer. "All right," he said, and stumbled off drowsily down the stairs.

VI *An Engineer for Bertram*

Freddy's invention of pockets for animals had not really been a success. On his trip he had interested a good many animals in them, partly because he was a high-class salesman and partly because they were such a new idea. But once the novelty wore off, the animals forgot about them and stopped wearing them.

"Trouble is," said Freddy, one warm May day when he and Georgie and Jock, the collie, were resting on the bank of the duck pond after a dip, "most animals have got along without carrying things around with them all their lives, and so they don't really feel a need for pockets. If they'd been born with pockets, they'd use them."

"The way I feel about it," said Jock: "they're kind of hot and uncomfortable to wear all the time. But I would like them on a long trip. Only most animals don't take long trips."

"There comes Adoniram," said Georgie. He looked toward the barn, from which a figure came striding quickly toward them. Georgie's tail began to vibrate, and Jock's gave a couple of dignified thumps on the ground.

"You dogs are awfully lucky having tails that you can wag," said Freddy. "It's such an easy way of being polite. You don't have to say: 'How do you do? I'm glad to see you.' You just let your tails do it for you with a couple of wags. You know, when I was little I spent hours trying to wag my tail. But I couldn't move it. It never changes its expression at all, except to come uncurled a little when the weather's damp. What good is a tail like that?"

"It's ornamental," said Georgie. "It adds

something, Freddy, really. It sort of finishes you off, like a little flag."

"Finishes me off all right," said Freddy. "It's like the period at the end of a sentence—it shows where I come to an end.—Say, what's the matter with Adoniram? Why does he walk so funny?"

All three turned to look at the figure, now quite close to them. He was striding along with a queer, stiff gait, coming straight toward them, and making a funny clicking sound.

"Gosh!" said Freddy suddenly. "It isn't Adoniram. It's the clockwork boy. Uncle Ben's finished him.—Hey, look out, you! You'll go into the pond!"

But the figure strode straight through them as they rolled aside to avoid being stepped on, and went over the bank and into the water with a splash. "Stop him! Stop him!" shouted a voice, and they saw Uncle Ben come stumping along toward them as fast as his short legs would carry him.

Jock had jumped into the water, and Freddy and Georgie followed him. The clockwork boy was thrashing around in the pond, still making walking motions with his legs. He was dressed in

a suit of Adoniram's, and the animals finally caught hold of his coat-sleeves and dragged him in toward the bank.

"Leave him there," said Uncle Ben, who had come up by this time, "till he runs down."

"That's right," said Jock. "He can't drown, can he?" The collie climbed out, and the others followed him. They all looked at Uncle Ben.

Uncle Ben was evidently struggling with a thought. He had both hands buried in his whiskers and was tugging them frantically as he stared down at the figure, which was lying on its side with a placid smile on its face, as if entirely unaware of the furious activity of its legs. " 'Twon't work," said Uncle Ben at last.

"I should say it worked almost too well," said Freddy.

Uncle Ben shook his head. "Start him," he said, "can't stop him. Hadn't been for pond—been in Centerboro by now."

"That's right," said Freddy. "You've got to be able to stop him doing things after you start him. I never thought of that."

"No engineer," said Uncle Ben.

Most of Uncle Ben's conversation was like that.

He could put a whole sentence into two words. Some people found it difficult to understand what he was talking about, but Freddy had worked with him so long by now that he knew what the old man meant. "Of course," he said; "he's no more good this way than an automobile without someone to drive it. We've got to have somebody to run him."

"Animals too big," said Uncle Ben.

"Yes, even Georgie would be too big," said Freddy. "We'd have to build a place for him to sit inside, and—"

"How about Ronald," said Georgie. "He's small enough."

"Ha!" exclaimed Uncle Ben. "Rooster!" He drew a sheaf of plans out of his pocket, spread them out on the bank, and began studying them. After a few minutes he nodded his head, folded up the plans, and went up to the barn for a wheelbarrow. When he got back he dragged the clockwork boy out of the pond with the help of the animals, loaded him, still kicking, into the wheelbarrow, and took him up to the barn.

Freddy and the two dogs went over to the henhouse to talk to Ronald. The rooster was delighted with the idea of being engineer for the clockwork boy. "It'll be just like having an automobile," he said. "I can drive him to Centerboro —go anywhere I want to—"

"The idea is to have a playmate for Adoniram, remember," said Freddy. "Not just for you to have a lot of fun by yourself, and taking people for rides, and so on."

"Oh, quite," said Ronald. "You leave it to me. When do I get my first lesson?"

"You'd better go talk to Uncle Ben," said Jock.

It was several days before Uncle Ben completed the alterations which were necessary. But it was a nice job when it was done. There was a little door in the clockwork boy's back for Ronald to get in by, and a window just at one side of his necktie to look out through, and inside there was a perch for Ronald facing all the little levers that controlled the arms and hands and head and legs. And there was also a microphone rigged up so that Ronald could talk for him.

It took Ronald some time to learn how to work all the levers properly, for the boy was much more complicated to run than an automobile. Nothing had been said to Adoniram about all this, although most of the animals knew about it. So the first time Ronald took the boy out they waited until Adoniram had gone to bed.

It was a bright moonlight night. The clock-work boy stood in the doorway of the big red barn, surrounded by a ring of excited animals, while Uncle Ben wound him up good and tight. Then Ronald fluttered up into the little door and closed it behind him. He pulled a couple of levers and the boy put his hand over his heart and bowed to the animals.

"Quiet! Quiet!" said Freddy, as the animals started to raise a cheer. "Are you all right, Ronald?"

"O. K. Here we go!" boomed a great voice, that echoed back from the surrounding hills.

"Great Scott!" exclaimed Jinx. "We can't have a voice like that in him! Sounds more like a lion than a boy."

But Uncle Ben stepped forward, opened the little door, and, reaching in over Ronald's head, made a few adjustments in the microphone. "Now try."

"O.K. Here we go!" came a rather hollow, but much smaller voice.

"Well, it might be a boy's voice," said Freddy, "if the boy had a bad cold and was talking with his head in a barrel. But I guess it's all right."

"What's his name?" came the hollow voice again.

"That's right," said Freddy. "He's got to have a name. Well, Uncle Ben, he's your boy if he's anybody's. You name him."

"Bertram," said Uncle Ben without hesitation.

So then the animals stood back and Bertram walked slowly around the barnyard once, and then he ran around, and then he hippety-hopped around. By this time Ronald was pretty sure of himself, and he put Bertram through his paces. He closed the barn doors, and threw stones, and chased Jinx and caught him and pulled his tail, and did a lot of other stunts, and then he came up and shook hands with Uncle Ben.

Most of the animals thought that Ronald had done so well that Bertram could be introduced to Adoniram the next morning, but Uncle Ben said no, he'd got to have more practice. And it was lucky he did. For the next night Ronald took Bertram out again. And they had an accident.

It happened this way: Bertram had done a lot of stunts, and he was showing the animals how he was going to play ball with Adoniram. He was being a pitcher, and he was just showing them how he would deliver a fast one when his hand, which hadn't been screwed on very tight, flew off and sailed up in a big curve and went *Crash!* through Mr. Bean's bedroom window.

All the animals ducked for cover. They were horrified to see Bertram still standing there in the moonlight. "Beat it!" they whispered. "Go in the barn." But Bertram didn't move.

And then Mr. Bean's head appeared at the window. On his head was his white nightcap with the red tassel, and his left eye was closed and his right eye was squinting down the barrel of his shotgun.

"Halt! Who goes there!" he shouted.

Now, Bertram hadn't run away because when he wound up to pitch the imaginary ball his necktie had slid over the little window, and Ronald couldn't see out. But he heard Mr. Bean's voice, and he was so scared that he just opened the little door and jumped out and ran.

Mr. Bean saw the rooster quite clearly in the moonlight. "Ha! Chicken-thieves, eh?" he shouted, and he aimed at Bertram's legs and pulled the trigger. There was a loud bang and the rattle of shot, but of course they didn't hurt Bertram any. "Well, I'll be switched!" said Mr. Bean. "I know I hit him, but he never jumped. Well—" and he pumped another cartridge in and pulled the trigger.

Bang! And this time one of the shot somehow hit the lever that made Bertram walk. He started off toward the gate, and he walked into the gate and knocked it flat and went on into the side of the cow-barn with a loud crash, and his head fell off. And at that Mr. Bean gave a loud yell and slammed down the window.

For a minute there was a complete silence. Then from the shadow of the barn doorway where Uncle Ben was standing came a queer, rusty, creaking sound and Uncle Ben came out into the moonlit barnyard and danced around, waving his arms and stamping until he looked like a gnome out of some old fairy-tale book, and all the time that queer, wheezy, rusty sound came out of him. I think Freddy was the first who realized it was the sound of Uncle Ben laughing.

Under the sound of the laughter Freddy could make out faint rustlings and scrapings, which was the sound of the other animals all sneaking off to bed. But he and Jinx stayed hidden in the little tool-shed where they had taken refuge, and pretty soon Uncle Ben calmed down and went up to the house. After a minute a light went on in the kitchen and for quite a while there was a rumble of voices, as Uncle Ben explained to Mr. Bean what had happened. Then Uncle Ben came out again, followed by Mr. Bean in his nightcap, long white nightshirt, and carpet slippers, carrying a lantern. The two men were both laughing now. They went down and picked up Bertram and stuck his head back on and carried him up into the loft. Then they went back into the house.

"Well," said Jinx, "I guess the party's over. Gosh, Mr. Bean must have been scared when he saw the chicken-thief's head fall off. Ho, hum. Good night, Freddy."

"Good night, Jinx." And the two animals went off to bed.

VII *Adoniram's Uncle Comes For Him*

Uncle Ben repaired Bertram the next morning, and at noon Ronald hopped into the control room and drove the clockwork boy up to the house to meet Adoniram. Bertram shook hands with the boy, and with Mr. and Mrs. Bean, and walked and ran and sat down and threw stones and showed some of the things he could do.

"Land sakes!" said Mrs. Bean, "you'd swear the creature was alive. What won't Uncle Ben think up next!"

"The Beans are a smart family, Mrs. B.," said her husband.

"It takes you to say it," said Mrs. Bean.

"Yes, sir," said Mr. Bean, "smart's the word for 'em. But I can only think of one of 'em that ever did anything smarter than what Uncle Ben's done with this Bertram."

"And what was that, Mr. B.?"

"That was when I married you," said the farmer, and slapped Mrs. Bean on the shoulder.

"Get along with you!" said Mrs. Bean blushing, and then she turned to Adoniram and said: "Well, how do you like him?"

"Oh, I think he's grand," said the boy. "We can have lots of fun together."

"How about going fishing this afternoon, Adoniram?" said Bertram.

Adoniram was delighted with the idea, and he ran and got the poles and dug some worms, and he and Bertram strode off down the road together, talking and laughing as happily as if they were really two boys going fishing.

The animals had all gathered by the back door to see Bertram presented to the family, and now several of them started after the boys. But Mr.

Bean called to them to stop. "You animals mind your own business. You're going to have plenty of chances to look at Bertram without chasing after him now. What fun do you think Adoniram'll have fishing if there's an animal hiding in every bush? I know what it was like, that time you were all playing detective, and I couldn't move a blade of grass without finding a pig or a rabbit under it. Leave 'em alone." And he picked up his hoe and started for the garden.

But Mrs. Bean stopped him. "Before you go," she said, "did you see this letter that came this morning? It's from Adoniram's folks, but I didn't want to speak about it in front of him."

Mr. Bean took the letter, put on a pair of very small steel spectacles, and read the letter through once upside down, and then he read it through right side up, and then he scratched his head and said: "Shucks!"

"They're comin' for him tomorrow," said Mrs. Bean.

"What!" exclaimed Uncle Ben.

"They won't let us adopt him," said Mrs. Bean. "They want him back."

"Fury!" said Uncle Ben.

"Nothing we can do, Mrs. B.," said Mr. Bean. "They got the rights of it, seemingly. Poor boy! I was gettin' right fond of him, too."

"Well, they shan't have him back," said Mrs. Bean, getting very red. It was the first time any of the animals had ever seen her angry. "Horrid, cruel people! I won't give him up. I—"

"Now, now, Mrs. B.," said her husband, "no use gettin' het up over it. I talked it all over with Mr. Jerks, the attorney, over to Centerboro, and he says—"

"I don't care what your old attorney says," burst out Mrs. Bean. "That boy's *not going back!* Not if I have to get that old shotgun of yours and drive 'em off."

Uncle Ben and Mr. Bean looked at each other and pursed up their lips, and then they looked around at the ring of interested animals. "We mustn't get the wrong side of the law," said Mr. Bean at last. "Just the same, it seems as if we ought to be able to think up *something*. After all, we got a whole day. You animals," he said suddenly "—what's the matter with you all? You're smart—you've got the name of being the smartest animals in York State. Well—prove it! Get to thinking. Hold a meeting. Hold six meetings. But think of something before tomorrow.

"Wait a minute," he added, as the animals started to walk away, all trying very hard to look thoughtful. "Remember, we don't want to hurt these people. But remember, too, that animals can do things that humans can't. If we drive these folks away, they'll just go get the sheriff and maybe arrest us. But the law can't touch animals. —Now, go think!"

The amount of thinking that a couple of dozen farm animals can do in an afternoon is quite surprising. By supper time, when Adoniram and Bertram came back with a nice string of yellow perch, they had thought of sixteen separate plans. The meeting they held in the barn that night was one of the hottest debates in the history of the Bean farm. They voted and voted, and at last at midnight, when several animals had fainted from excitement and had to be carried outside, and Charles had spoken until he was so hoarse he could no longer be heard, a plan was adopted. It wasn't a very good plan, but it seemed the best of the sixteen.

The following day scouts were posted on the

hills overlooking the road by which Adoniram's relatives were expected to arrive. Adoniram had been got out of the way by sending him and Bertram off to Centerboro in the phaeton, drawn by Hank. Mr. Bean had given them each fifty cents and told them to have a good time, and he had privately told Hank not to get them back before supper.

At two o'clock a handkerchief fluttered on the top of Swan Hill, and was answered from half a dozen other heights, and from the roof of the Bean house, where two squirrels were keeping watch. Adoniram's uncle and aunt, rattling along eastward in their old car, saw nothing unusual in the peaceful countryside until, about two miles from the Bean farm, they came upon three cows standing in the middle of the road, who lowered their horns threateningly as the car came to a stop.

Adoniram's uncle got out and picked up a stick to drive the cows away, but as he did so eight skunks came out of the bushes and advanced upon him. These were Sniffy Wilson and his family, who had volunteered for the first line of defence. Adoniram's uncle bounced back into the car as if he had springs in his heels. But instead of turning around, as the animals had expected, he swung out into the ditch around the cows, knocked over Snuffy, Sniffy's little brother, and two seconds later was roaring on up the road.

"Well, that's that," said Mrs. Wiggins. "He's got more spunk than I thought he'd have."

"He isn't a man that gives up easy," said Mrs. Wurzburger. "I'm afraid he'll get Adoniram yet."

"Well, so long, girls," called Sniffy. "Sorry we had no better luck. But if you need us again, we're ready." And they dove back into the bushes. The cows followed along after the car at a trot, and a quarter of a mile farther on came up with it. It had stopped again, and Adoniram's uncle was working at a small tree which had fallen across the road. Freddy had hired a couple of beavers to cut it down that morning.

"Look out," yelled Adoniram's aunt, "here comes those cows!"

The man turned to face them, and at that moment out of the bushes burst a dozen animals— horses, sheep, a goat, and Peter, the big bear from down in the woods. They closed in on Adoniram's uncle, and Peter held him while Jinx, who was clever at knots, tied him up tight with a length of clothesline.

"Load him in the car, boys," yelled Jinx. "We'll drag them down to the river and give 'em a good ducking. We'll teach 'em to be mean to little boys! We'll send 'em back where they came from."

Now this part of the plan would probably have worked all right, and Adoniram's aunt and uncle would probably have been so thoroughly scared by the behavior of such wild animals that they would never have ventured into that part of the country again. But they had thought there might be trouble in getting Adoniram back, so they had brought along a gun. They weren't very nice people.

The first thing the animals knew about the gun, there was a bang, and the whistle of a bullet over their heads. Fortunately, Adoniram's aunt wasn't a very good shot, so she didn't hit anybody. But there was nothing for any sensible animal to do but run. In three seconds after the report there wasn't an animal in sight.

Adoniram's aunt got out and untied her husband, and after he had danced up and down the road for a few minutes in his rage, he got back into the car and they drove on. And pretty soon they came to the Bean farm.

Everything was quiet around the farm; not even a chicken was in sight. The car drew up at the gate, and Adoniram's uncle started to get out, and then stopped suddenly. For on the gate was a large sign: "MEASLES."

"Look at this," he said. "I can't go in here. I never had measles."

"You had German measles," said his wife.

"It ain't the same thing," he said. "Anyway, what's the use of arguing? You've had both kinds. Get out and go in and get Adoniram."

So after quite an argument she got out and went in the gate.

But in less than a minute she was back again.

"There's another sign on the door," she said. "It says 'Scarlet fever.' I never had scarlet fever, but you did, so I guess you'll have to go in."

"I can't go in," said Adoniram's uncle. "This sign says 'Measles' and I never had measles."

"You had German measles," said Adoniram's aunt. And the argument began all over again.

All around the barnyard, behind trees and

bushes and sheds and fences, the animals were hidden, and as the argument went on and on and got hotter and hotter, they squirmed and panted and stuffed grass in their mouths to keep from laughing out loud. But pretty soon Adoniram's uncle got so mad at Adoniram's aunt that he slapped her, and then she pulled his hair, and then they fought each other until they were out of breath. And at last Adoniram's uncle said: "Well, all right. We won't either of us go in. No use wasting time here. We'll go down to Centerboro and telephone. If Adoniram's got something catching, we'll have to come for him again when he gets well." And he started up the engine and drove off.

"Darn it," said Freddy, "wouldn't you think it would be enough for them just to see the signs? If they call up, Mrs. Bean'll tell 'em that Adoniram isn't sick, and then they'll come back."

"I could stick around and answer the phone when it rings," said Jinx, "if you can get Mrs. Bean out of the house for a while. Can't you have a fit or faint away or something?"

"Hey, look, Freddy," said Georgie. "Hadn't somebody ought to warn Adoniram? I mean, if these people go to Centerboro, they might see him."

"Good gracious, I never thought of that," said the pig. "But we can't get there before they do."

"I could," said Ferdinand, who was sitting on the fence, listening to the conversation.

"Main Street in Centerboro is no place for a crow, Ferdinand. You know that. But wait a minute. How about that friend of yours, Jinx, that wasp—what's his name? Fellow that came in first in that free-for-all insects' cross-country run last year."

"Jacob?" said Jinx. "Sure, he'd go. I'll get him," and Jinx dashed off.

"All right," said Freddy. "That fixes that. Now I'm going to faint. No giggling, you fellows." And he walked out into the middle of the barnyard, gave a loud squeal, and fell over on his back with all four feet in the air.

Meanwhile Jacob, swiftly instructed by Jinx, crawled out of his nest under the eaves of the barn, saw that his sting was in working order— "because you never know," he said, "when you may have to fight your way out of a tight spot"— and took flight. He spiraled up until he was over the barn, and then, with all four wings whirring, aimed like a bullet for Centerboro church spire.

He had gone about four miles when he saw below him on the road Adoniram's aunt and uncle chugging along in the same direction. He overhauled them swiftly, then swooped down and flew just above them for a way, listening to their conversation.

"You wait till I get my hands on him," Adoniram's uncle was saying. "I'll bet he won't try to run away again."

"I wonder how he'll like being locked up in the cellar on bread and water for a week," said Adoniram's aunt.

Jacob swooped down and lit on the seat just behind them. He took out his sting and polished it on the upholstery and looked longingly at the back of Adoniram's uncle's neck. But then he shook his head regretfully. "Mustn't exceed orders," he said. And he rose with an angry buzz that made them both duck, and flew on.

Jacob flew up and down Main Street, looking in the windows of bakeries and candy stores for Bertram and Adoniram. They weren't anywhere in sight. But at the curb in front of the Centerboro Cinema Palace he saw the old phaeton with Hank asleep between the shafts. So he flew into the theater.

It was very dark inside after the sunlit street and he couldn't see a thing. He flew down the aisle, buzzing rather loudly in his nervousness, and several people crouched down and said: "Look out! There's a wasp in here," and one old lady made a pass at him and hit the man next to her on the ear. The man hadn't heard Jacob, and he was naturally surprised, and gave the old lady a shove. Then he saw that she was an old lady and started to apologize, but by that time the old lady was mad, so she hit him again, and another man behind him, who had seen him shove the old lady, also hit him. And then the first man got really mad and hit the second man, and everybody shouted: "Quiet, quiet! Throw them out!" And two more men joined in, and in about two minutes half the people in the theater were arguing and shoving each other, and five fights had started. But Jacob was sitting on the big chandelier above it all, looking for Adoniram.

Pretty soon the noise got so bad that the movie stopped and the lights went on. A lot of people were starting for the door, and among them Jacob at last saw the two he was looking for. There was no use trying to get Adoniram's attention, so he dropped down and lit on Bertram's necktie and leaned out and waved his feelers in front of the little window to attract Ronald's attention.

"Wait a minute, Adoniram," said Ronald, and he pulled some levers and Bertram sat down in a seat and Adoniram sat down beside him. Then he opened the door and let Jacob in, and after he had heard the news, he told the boy about it. "You stay here," he said, "and I'll go outside and scout around."

By now the people had quieted down and the show had started again, so Adoniram was perfectly willing to stay. Ronald steered Bertram out and woke Hank up and told him to go around into a back street. "Then," he said, "I'll sneak Adoniram out and we'll take the back road home."

He had just finished talking to Hank when rattling down Main Street came the car containing Adoniram's relatives. And then Ronald made a mistake. They were not looking for him, he knew, and he had forgotten that Bertram's face looked exactly like Adoniram's. So he didn't move. And Adoniram's aunt saw him.

"There he is now!" she yelled, and jumped right out of the car and grabbed him by the arm.

"Gosh, what'll I do?" said Ronald to the wasp. He had to whisper so it wouldn't be Bertram that spoke. "Shall I run? They couldn't possibly hold on to Bertram."

"You can always get away later," said Jacob. "Get in with them. You'll be leading them away from Adoniram."

"You get into the car, you wicked little wretch," said Adoniram's aunt. "I'll teach you to run away from home." And she gave him a slap. And then she gave a yell of pain, for of course Bertram's cheek was made of wood.

When he saw his wife hopping around and shaking her hurt hand, Adoniram's uncle got mad, and he jumped out and bundled Bertram into the back seat of the car. "You will strike your aunt, will you?" he said vindictively. "You just wait till we get home, young man." And he backed the car around and started off up the street.

"I don't like this much," whispered Ronald.

"Don't be silly," said Jacob. "They can't do a thing to you. It's just as if you were in a fort. No, you stick it out awhile. I'll fly back and report at the farm, and then I'll come tell you what they say."

"Well, Adoniram saved my life," said Ronald doubtfully, "so I suppose I ought to do what I can."

"That's the spirit," said the wasp. "Well, so long. Don't worry. I'll be back."

"So long," said Ronald as he opened the little door. Then he gave a deep sigh and settled himself firmly on his perch.

VIII *Bertram Visits Snare Forks*

Adoniram's uncle kept his foot hard down on the accelerator, for they had a long way to go, and they wanted to get home that night. The car leaped and bounced, and Ronald had to hang on tight and didn't have a chance to do much thinking. He did enough, though, to decide that there really wasn't anything to worry about. They had been going about two hours when Jacob came back. He signaled through the window, and Ronald let him in.

"I've talked to the animals," said the wasp,

"and they think that if you'll stick with Bertram for just a few days, then you can escape and drive him back home. And probably Adoniram's folks will get discouraged if he runs away again and let the Beans adopt him."

"That's all right," said Ronald, "but I haven't been married very long. One can't desert one's bride practically at the altar, you know, and go careering off in search of adventure."

"Oh, I talked to Cackletta," said Jacob. "She said she thought it was just wonderful of you to do this for Adoniram. She said she thought you were terribly brave. And you'd have such marvelous adventures to tell her about when you got back."

There never yet was a rooster that couldn't be flattered into doing something he didn't want to do. Ronald puffed out his chest and tried at the same time to look modest, which is practically impossible. "Oh, I say!" he said. "Nothing brave about it, you know, old man. Line of duty. Have to do these things, what? Thought it was brave of me, eh?"

"Brave as a lion."

"Silly little thing!" said Ronald tenderly.

"Well, well, you can tell them that I shall try to live up to their expectations. Never fear, I will return triumphant."

"England expects every man to do his duty, eh?" said Jacob. "That's the stuff. Well, I must push off. If we don't hear from you inside a week, we'll know you can't get away, and Jinx said in that case don't worry—the gang will come after you. So long."

Ronald had talked so bravely that he began to feel brave—which is something that quite often happens to people. At six o'clock Adoniram's uncle and aunt stopped at a restaurant and had supper. They told Bertram that he couldn't have anything to eat, but must stay in the car. But as Bertram never ate anything anyway this was no punishment. As for Ronald, he had a box of corn meal in the control room, so it wasn't any hardship for him either.

It was after midnight when they got back to the house by the river. There was some discussion whether they should spank Bertram then or wait until morning, but they were both pretty tired so they decided to postpone it, feeling they wouldn't do justice to it unless they were fresh.

So they sent him down to the barn to bed.

When Ronald got Bertram into the barn he opened the door and hopped out and stretched his wings, and at first he thought he would spend the night perched on a tree outside, for the night was warm and close. But then he decided he had better not, for if he overslept after his long ride, and Adoniram's uncle came down to the barn before he could get back into the control room, they might think Bertram was sick and send for a doctor. And then of course they would find out that he was a clockwork boy, and not Adoniram at all.

So Ronald had Bertram walk over to a window and turn his back to it, and then he opened the little door so the breeze would blow on him, and went to sleep. And Bertram stood up all night.

Early in the morning the rooster was awakened by a shout of "Adoniram!" He shook the sleep out of his eyes and pulled the right levers, and Bertram turned around and walked out of the barn.

"Oh," said Adoniram's uncle, "you're up and dressed, are you? Wonder you wouldn't answer when you're called."

"I'm sorry, sir, I didn't hear," said Ronald.

"Eh? What's the matter with your voice, boy?" said the man, staring at him in surprise.

"Got a cold," said Ronald, and, to prove it, wiped his sleeve across his nose.

"Use your handkerchief!" said the man.

"I haven't got one," said Ronald.

"That's a fine excuse, that is," said the other. "Well, take the hoe and go down and hoe the potatoes for an hour while I have my breakfast. Then come back here and I'll give you your spanking. Then your aunt will give you your breakfast, and then she will spank you, and then you can go back to the potatoes."

"Yes, sir," said Ronald, and Bertram got a hoe and strode off toward the potato patch.

Adoniram's uncle looked after him curiously. "Wonder why he walks so stiff," he said to himself. "Can't be rheumatism at his age. Well, maybe a good whipping will limber him up."

Bertram hoed for an hour, and as he never had to stop for a rest, he did as much hoeing as four men would have done in the time. The hoeing had been rather fun for Ronald, but "I don't know," he said as he went back to the house for his spanking; "if Bertram does as much work as that they'll never let him get away again."

"Now, young man," said Adoniram's uncle, "get across my knee."

Bertram knelt down and leaned his weight on the man's knees.

"Quit making that clicking noise," said Adoniram's uncle. "Good land, you've put on a lot of weight. Been havin' too much to eat, likely. Well, we'll see if you get any fatter on bread and water." Then he started to spank.

But he didn't spank very long. In fact, after the first spank he gave a yell and shook his fingers as his wife had done after she had slapped Bertram. Only it hurt him worse, because his hand had come down on one of the iron hinges that joined Bertram's legs to his body.

"Get up, consarn you!" he roared. "I'll teach you to put bricks under your clothes. Luella, where's the horsewhip?"

So Adoniram's aunt brought the horsewhip, and Adoniram's uncle whipped Bertram until he was pretty nearly exhausted. And Ronald made whining noises every time the whip fell, so it would sound as if it hurt. Ronald enjoyed himself quite a lot at first. But then he remembered that this whipping was really intended for Adoniram, who was his friend, and he got mad. At first he thought he'd make Bertram hit Adoniram's uncle, but he was afraid that they might put him in jail if he did that. So he thought a minute, and then he remembered how Uncle Ben had adjusted the microphone, so he turned it up to make it louder, and yelled: "Ouch! You're hurting me! Ow-ow-ow!"

Well, you know what happens when you turn the radio on too loud. That was just what happened to Bertram. Adoniram's aunt and uncle yelled and ran outdoors, and farmers plowing on distant hillsides and housewives washing up the breakfast dishes stopped work and looked up and said: "My goodness, somebody bein' killed? Over toward the Smith place, seemin'ly."

Ronald bawled for quite a while, but at last he stopped and went to the door. Adoniram's uncle and aunt were whispering to each other and they were as white as two sheets. They stopped when they saw him.

"Don't you ever make such a noise again," said

126

Adoniram's aunt coming toward him. "My goodness, what will the neighbors think?"

"We won't whip you any more," said Adoniram's uncle.

So Ronald turned the microphone down and said: "All right."

"Go in and eat your bread and water," said Adoniram's aunt.

"I don't want anything to eat," said Bertram, and he picked up his hoe and went back to the potato patch.

But this time he didn't do any work at all. He leaned the hoe against a tree and sat down in the grass. Pretty soon he heard a shout: "Adoniraaaam!" But he didn't move. And presently Adoniram's uncle came along.

"Get up," he said, and when Bertram still didn't move, Adoniram's uncle kicked him. And, of course, hurt his toe.

"See here boy," he said when he had stopped hopping around, "there's some things you've got to understand. One is, you're going to work on this farm like you used to do. And the other is, if you try any more monkey business of putting stones in your pockets, I'll give you a beating you won't forget."

Bertram turned the microphone up again and said: "What?" in a voice that could have been heard six miles.

"Quiet!" said Adoniram's uncle, looking around apprehensively. "All right, I won't whip you again. But you've got to do your work. If you don't, you just won't get fed, that's all."

"That's all right with me," said Bertram.

"What!" exclaimed Adoniram's uncle. "You dare say that to me?"

But Ronald had learned how to talk to him. He turned the microphone up again and bawled: "I won't eat and I won't work!" And Adoniram's uncle put his hands over his ears and ran.

"Well, what happens next, I wonder?" said Ronald to himself. But what happened was a pretty big surprise. For Bertram hadn't been wound up since the morning of the previous day. And suddenly he ran down and fell over flat on his back.

Ronald was in real trouble now. For the little door he got in and out by was in Bertram's back, and he couldn't open it. He got hold of the key that wound Bertram up, but he wasn't strong enough to turn it. And then he thought for a while, but that didn't do any good either, because the only thought he had was that he had been a fool to come.

But after Bertram had lain there for an hour or so, Adoniram's aunt came out to see if she couldn't shame him into working.

"You big lazy hulk," she said, "aren't you ashamed of yourself, lying there with all this work to be done!"

"I'm sick," said Bertram weakly. "I can't get up."

She stared at him, frowning. "Well, what do you expect," she said, "if you won't eat your breakfast?"

So she stood and argued with him for a while, and then as he still said he was too weak to get up, she went and called her husband.

"If he's really sick," she said, "we must get him in the house."

So Adoniram's uncle leaned down to get hold of him.

"No, no, it hurts," said Bertram. "Don't touch me." For Ronald was afraid that if they tried to carry Bertram, they'd find out what he really was.

"Have to call a doctor, I guess," said Adoniram's uncle.

"Nonsense," said his wife. "Spend good money on doctor's bills for a worthless lump of a boy? I guess not! I guess you wish you'd let those people adopt him now. What good is he?"

So they argued for a while, and at last agreed to call the doctor.

Dr. Murdock was a red-faced old gentleman with white whiskers and glasses that kept falling off. "Well, well, well," he said when he saw Bertram, "what have we here?" And he felt of Bertram's wrist. "Pulse very feeble," he said. "Looks like starvation to me." And he stared very hard at Adoniram's uncle and aunt.

They both started explaining at once, how the boy had refused his breakfast, and how they always fed him well, and how good they were to him.

"Yes, yes, yes," said Dr. Murdock impatiently. "I know all about that. I heard him yelling this morning when I stopped in to see old Mrs. Scrunch's rheumatism. Guess you licked him a little too hard, eh?"

Then he bent down and put his ear to Bertram's chest to listen to his heart.

"Doctor," whispered Ronald. "I want to tell you something. Send them away."

Dr. Murdock started violently when he heard this whisper coming out of a chest where a heart should have been beating. But like most doctors, he was never very much surprised at anything he found inside his patients, and when he had recovered his glasses, which had fallen off when he jumped, he sent Adoniram's uncle and aunt away. They didn't want to go very much, but he made them.

"Turn me over, doctor," said Ronald, and with a good deal of heaving and grunting, and remarks about what a husky boy Adoniram was, to be sure, the doctor turned him on his face. And Ronald opened the door and came out.

Well, this did surprise Dr. Murdock, for he had never found a rooster in any of his patients before. "Upon my soul!" he exclaimed. "A rooster!"

"Yes, sir," said Ronald. And then he told the doctor the whole story.

"Humph," said the doctor when he had finished. "Well, there's one thing I'll say: you're the easiest case to cure I ever had." And he took hold of the key and wound Bertram up. "How long do you plan to stay here?"

"I don't know," said Ronald. "I expect I could go back most any time now. I don't suppose they'll come for Adoniram again, do you? After this?"

"I shouldn't think so," said Dr. Murdock. "I should think they'd be glad to have this Mr. Bean adopt him. But I don't know. They're mean people. I think if you could stay a few more days, so they will realize thoroughly that there's no more work to be got out of you—and maybe you'll think up some other ways of being disagreeable. They've mistreated that boy shamefully. They deserve any unpleasantness you can make for them. And, of course, I'll tell them that I have to see you every day for a few days—so I can come over and keep Bertram, here, wound up, you see?"

So then Ronald got back into the control room and showed Dr. Murdock a few of the things Bertram could do, and then the doctor went up to the house.

Adoniram's aunt and uncle were pretty mad at

having to pay the doctor, especially as he said the boy oughtn't to do any work for a while. They tried to make Bertram do some more hoeing that afternoon, but he just refused and went off and took a walk. The next day was about the same, and in the afternoon Dr. Murdock came and wound Bertram up. And that evening Adoniram's uncle and aunt came down to the barn.

They came very quietly, an hour after Bertram had gone to bed, but Ronald heard them coming. Roosters have small ears, but they don't miss much. Bertram was standing by the window again, but Ronald had him lie down quickly, and Bertram's adjustable eyelids clicked shut. And when Adoniram's aunt bent over to look at him, Ronald made sleeping sounds.

"Psst!" said Adoniram's aunt, and Adoniram's uncle rushed in with a lantern and a clothes-line and quickly tied Bertram's arms tight to his sides while his wife knotted a towel over his mouth so he couldn't yell.

"And now," said Adoniram's uncle, reaching for the whip, "get up on your feet, Adoniram. I've spanked you with hands and hairbrushes and basting spoons and I've licked you with shingles and carriage whips and dust mops and I've whaled you with straps and broom handles and yardsticks and old pieces of pipe. But after all that, you're just the same stubborn, good-for-nothing, lazy lummox you always were. So I'm going to give you the most everlasting high-powered father and mother of a lambasting you ever had in your life. And then I guess you'll do as you're told. Take off your coat."

Now Bertram couldn't take his coat off when his hands were tied, and anyway Ronald knew that if he did, a lot of machinery would be visible. While he got Bertram to his feet he was wondering what to do. "I guess," he said to himself, "that now is the time to take the doctor's advice and be kind of unpleasant." So as Adoniram's uncle swung the whip back, Bertram just raised his arms, and the clothes line snapped like string and dropped to the floor.

"Look out!" yelled Adoniram's aunt, and ran for the door. Her husband dashed after her, and before Bertram could follow they had slammed the heavy barn door shut and wedged it tight with a piece of timber.

"There," shouted Adoniram's uncle, "now

we'll see who's master around here. You'll stay there until you're ready to do as you're told." And they both laughed nastily.

But Bertram walked up to the door and drew back his fists and punched—right, left, right, left—and each time a fist went splintering right through the planks. When they were pretty well weakened, he put his shoulder against them and pushed, and then he was out in the open, walking slowly along after his two persecutors, who were scuttling off toward the house.

The front door was locked when he got to the house, but he just walked into it and it went down—bang! He heard a squeal of fright, and footsteps racing up the stairs. He followed them. Everything was quiet on the second floor. But all the doors were open except the one to the attic stairs. He kicked that down and went up the stairs—clump, clump, clump. And there, cowering behind a trunk, he found them.

He reached out one hand and caught Adoniram's uncle by the collar and pulled him out. Adoniram's uncle struggled and hit out, but he only hit Bertram on the nose and bruised his knuckles. He didn't even chip the paint. And

Bertram caught him by the waist and swung him up and hung him by the coat collar on a big hook that was screwed into one of the rafters.

"Let me down," roared Adoniram's uncle. "I was only whipping you for your own good, Adoniram. It hurt me worse than it did you."

"I guess it did, at that," said Bertram.

"Oh, don't hurt him," begged Adoniram's aunt. "We'll promise not to whip you again. We'll do whatever you want us to."

"We don't want to make you do anything you don't want to do," said her husband. "We'll even let those Bean people adopt you, if you say so."

Well, this was just what Ronald wanted them to say. But he thought he'd have a little more fun before he left. "I don't know," he said doubtfully. "After all, you're my aunt and uncle. I expect probably I'd better stay here."

"But we're *not* your aunt and uncle," said Mrs. Smith. (I suppose we'd better call her that now, since she was really not Adoniram's aunt at all.) "We really haven't any claim on you at all, so if the Beans want you, for mercy's sake go live with them."

Ronald was pretty puzzled at this. You can see

why. He was Ronald, pretending to be Bertram, who was in turn pretending to be Adoniram. And now Adoniram was somebody else.

"Well, then," he said, "who am I?"

"There was a flood six years ago, almost as bad as the one this spring," said Mrs. Smith, "and you came floating down on a barn. We rescued you. You were too little to know where you came from, but you told us your name was Adoniram. You said you had another name, beginning with R, but you wouldn't ever tell us what it was. That's all we know."

"But didn't you ever try to find my people?"

"How could we?" said Mrs. Smith. "We're too busy to go traipsing around the country looking for them. If they wanted you, why didn't they look for you themselves?"

"You wanted to keep me so I could work for you when I grew up, I guess."

"Well, what if we did? We saved your life, didn't we? And a fine, grateful boy you turned out to be! Well, go your own way. We'll be glad to be rid of you."

"Oh, stop talking," groaned Mr. Smith, "and

let me down. Let him go, Luella, and a good riddance."

So Bertram lifted Mr. Smith down from the hook, and then they went downstairs and signed the papers that would let the Beans adopt Adoniram, and Bertram put them in his pocket and walked out of the house.

He went first to Dr. Murdock's and told him the whole story, and Dr. Murdock said he'd make inquiries and see if he could find out who Adoniram's parents really were. And then he wound up Bertram good and tight.

"You've got a long way to go," he said, "and you'll have to get wound up several times on the road, unless you're lucky enough to get a lift all the way. So I'd advise you to appeal to a policeman when you find yourself running down. They'll wind you up without any nonsense and you can trust them. Good-by and good luck."

Ronald had pretty good luck. He had gone barely half a mile when he came up to a car at the roadside. There was a man sitting on the running board.

"Hello, boy," he said. "I don't suppose you

know where I can find a jack around here, do you? I've got a flat tire, and no jack to lift the axle, and none of these cars that are going by will stop so I can borrow one."

"I guess I can help you," said Bertram. And he caught hold of the rear bumper and lifted the wheel clear of the ground. "I'll hold it while you get your spare tire on."

The man stared. "Great Scott, boy!" he exclaimed. "You ought to be in a circus. You ain't human!"

"You're right, I'm not," said Bertram. "But hurry. I can't hold this all day."

So the man put the tire on, and in return gave Bertram a lift for about fifty miles.

After that, Bertram walked for a mile or so more, and then he heard a horn blowing continuously behind him, coming nearer, and a big truck passed him and then drew up at the side of the road. The horn kept on blowing, and the driver got out and began poking around under the hood. "Guess I can't fix it," he said disconsolately as Bertram came up. "I'll have to let her blow. Don't dare shut it off altogether and drive without any horn at all."

"If you'll give me a lift, I'll be your horn," said Ronald, and he turned up the microphone and said: "Oo-hoo! Oo-hoooo!"

"Gosh," said the truckman, "that's a trick and a half, that is. That's odd trick *and* rubber. Get aboard, boy. I'll take you anywhere this side of Albany."

So Bertram got aboard. When the truckman wanted to pass anybody, he just said: "Horn," and Ronald would blow. And in between whiles they talked. The truckman wanted to learn how to make the horn noise, because he said he was pretty good at imitations, but Ronald said he didn't really know how he did it himself. Then the truckman did some of his imitations, and one of them was an imitation of a rooster.

"I can do a rooster myself," said Ronald, and he crowed.

"Pretty good," said the truckman. "Not bad at all. But listen, try to make it more like this."

Late in the afternoon Bertram got down from the truck, and he was within three miles of home.

He thanked the driver, and then he said: "There's just one thing. Do you still think your imitation of a rooster is better than mine?"

"Now listen, buddy," said the man. "Your imitation is good, all right. But you need practice. I've been doing it for years. It stands to reason mine's better."

"All right," said Ronald. "Now watch." He turned Bertram's back to the truckman, and then he stuck his head out of the little door and crowed. Then he shut the door and Bertram walked off up the hill road toward the Bean farm. But at the top of the hill he turned. The truck was still standing in the middle of the road, and seven cars were lined up behind it, blowing their horns to get by. But the truckman just sat motionless on his seat, staring after Bertram with his mouth open. And Ronald turned up the microphone and gave one last, trumpet-like crow, then waved his arm and went on over the brow of the hill.

And by and by the truckman shivered and threw in the clutch and drove on. But he never did any imitations again.

IX Mr. Boomschmidt Takes a Hand

Ronald was a pretty popular rooster after he got back. A big banquet in celebration was given in the barn, and the animals for miles around turned out to do him honor. Afterwards he made a speech and told about his adventures, and Cackletta, who sat beside him, was so proud that she cried all through it. When he finished there was prolonged cheering, and then Charles hopped up on to the dashboard of the phaeton and said:

"Ladies and gentlemen, friends and fellow-animals—" But before he could get any further,

Jinx reached up a claw and pulled him down.

"Shut up, Charles," he said. "Freddy has got something to say first."

"But I want to make a speech," said Charles. "I want to respond on behalf of the—the management. I always make that speech, Jinx."

"You always talk too much," said the cat. "Let Freddy speak, will you?"

"I don't see why Freddy should speak," said Charles stubbornly. "After all, Ronald is my son-in-law, a fellow-rooster—" He stopped, for Henrietta had pushed her way forward.

"And here's a fellow-hen that says you'd better come down off your perch and keep your beak shut," said Henrietta. "Come on, get down now."

"Oh, all right," said Charles, and he hopped down and shoved his way peevishly through the crowd toward the door.

"Ladies and gentlemen," said Freddy, getting up with some difficulty into the phaeton, "Mr. Benjamin Bean, whom we all know and love as Uncle Ben, has had an idea on which he has been working for some time and which I am sure you will agree is nothing short of a stroke of genius. He feels that conspicuous bravery should be re-

144

warded in some more tangible way than by mere applause, which so often is quickly forgotten. He feels that, in the case of such distinguished service as our friend Ronald has rendered, there should be some lasting token, some badge of honor, which will serve always to remind us of— of, well, such distinguished service. You will forgive my hesitation; I am no practiced orator like our friend Charles, here. And so, on behalf of Mrs. Bean and Mr. Bean and Uncle Ben and Adoniram and all the birds, animals, and insects here assembled, I take great pleasure in presenting you, Ronald, as a token of our gratitude and admiration, with the Benjamin Bean Distinguished Service Medal." And he flung over the rooster's head a ribbon at the end of which dangled a silver medal.

There were loud cheers, and the animals pressed forward to examine the trophy. Uncle Ben had done a nice job. On one side was a knight on horseback with an American flag in his hand, and on the other, Ronald's name, and the date, and the words: "Benjamin Bean Distinguished Service Medal. Presented for conspicuous bravery in the field."

While the animals, formed into a line, were filing by to see the medal and congratulate Ronald, suddenly Bertram, who had been standing motionless beside the phaeton, raised his arm, and in a voice which shook the rafters, shouted: "Ladies and gentlemen, attention, please!"

The noise was terrific. For a moment, shocked and frightened, the animals stared at Bertram, then they bolted for the door.

"It's Charles," said Georgie to Jinx. "I saw him sneak into the control room."

"The lunatic!" said the cat angrily. "He doesn't know how to run Bertram. Hey, Charles, cut it out. Get down out of there."

"Ha, ha, ha!" boomed Bertram. "Try and get me out, cat! I'm going to make my speech, and just try to stop me!" And his right arm made a wild swoop toward Jinx.

"Better get out of here," said Jinx. "We can't do anything till he comes out, and he might hurt somebody."

So Charles went on speaking. The barn was empty, but he didn't mind that. He knew that unless the animals left the farm entirely, they could hear every word he said. And as his speech boomed on, making the old barn tremble, and rolling out through the wide doorway into the night, to re-echo from the silent hills like thunder, he thought:

"Boy, what a magnificent speaking voice! If I only had a voice like that all the time, they'd *have* to listen to me."

Even Henrietta, perched on one of the rafters and clucking furiously at her husband, did not dare go too near Bertram. And she knew that Charles could not hear her. But resting on a couple of nails directly over Bertram's head was a pitchfork. The tremendous vibrations of the big voice jarred and shook it, and gradually it began to slide off its supports. "It is courage, my friends," roared Charles, "which we are rewarding tonight, the courage that fears nothing, that stands steadfast, in the face of surprise, of sudden attack—the courage, in short, of a rooster!" And at that the pitchfork slipped off the nails and came down on Bertram's head, knocking him flat on the floor.

The speech ended in a frightened squawk, the control room door popped open and out flew Charles. Henrietta was beside him instantly.

"Charles! Charles, are you hurt?"

"Where is he? Who did that?" demanded Charles belligerently. "Of course I'm not hurt. Who—"

"Then take that," said Henrietta, and boxed his left ear. "And that," she said, and boxed the right ear. "Courage of a rooster, eh? I'll give you something for your courage, you big noise. You're nothing but a loud speaker with tail-feathers. Get along home, or I'll—"

The animals didn't hear the rest of what she said, for Charles was in full retreat in the direction of the henhouse, and Henrietta was close after him. But they could hear her saying it for an hour or two more. Henrietta was a good forceful speaker, even though she never made speeches to anybody but her husband.

Adoniram was pretty happy after Ronald's return. He was glad to be adopted by the Beans, and he was glad, too, that the Smiths were not really his aunt and uncle.

"If I came down the river," he said to Georgie, "and if my name isn't Smith why maybe I really am the brother of your Byram. Wouldn't it be great to have a brother!"

"Well, personally," said Georgie, "I think you *are* brothers. I never saw two boys that looked more alike."

"Well," said Adoniram, "I expect we'll find him some day if we keep on looking. And in the meantime you like to be with me, don't you?"

"Sure I do," said the dog, wagging his tail as he looked up at the boy.

Adoniram thought for a minute. "I suppose," he said, "anybody that found Byram would rate one of those medals of Uncle Ben's, wouldn't he?"

"Golly," said Georgie, "that's an idea! These animals would do anything to get one of those medals. Let's go ask Uncle Ben."

Life on the Bean farm had been pretty strenuous since the presentation of the medal to Ronald. All the animals had gone around being brave, in the hope that they would get medals, but so far none had been awarded. Henrietta had come nearest it, for she had jumped into the pond to rescue a grasshopper. But then she had eaten the grasshopper, so that didn't count. Even the four mice, Eek and Quik and Eeny and Cousin Augustus, had been practicing up being brave by sitting at the doors of their holes and making faces at Jinx. At first Jinx didn't know what was the matter with them. He was sorry for them because he thought they had stomach-aches. And when they explained that they were insulting him, he just laughed.

When Adoniram spoke to Uncle Ben about offering the medal to anybody who could find Byram, the old man nodded. "Find him in a brave way—get the medal," he said.

"Yes, but suppose they aren't specially brave about it," said the boy. "I mean, suppose they just keep at it and keep at it until they find him."

"Persistence," said Uncle Ben. "No medal for persistence."

"Oh dear," said Adoniram. "Georgie and I thought it would be such a good way to get the animals to help find him."

Uncle Ben shook his head and went back to his bench. He was working now on an improved firecracker alarm clock, which, instead of firing just one cracker, fired a series of them, one every two minutes, each one louder than the last. Even the soundest sleeper couldn't sleep through the bang of the final giant cracker.

But the next day Uncle Ben called the boy up

into the loft and laid a medal in his hand. On one side was a bee, and the words: "Diligence, Persistence, Industry." On the other side it said: "The Adoniram Bean Diligence Medal. Awarded to —— for distinguished service and stick-to-it-iveness."

Adoniram was delighted with the medal. He thanked Uncle Ben and then ran out to tell the animals. But to his surprise, although they all said it was awfully nice and they hoped they could win it, none of them seemed very much excited.

"I tell you what's the matter," said Mrs. Wiggins. "Most people want to be thought brave, but they don't much care about being thought diligent. Or take it the other way round. Call any animal a coward and you'll make him madder'n a hornet. But call him lazy, and he'll just laugh. I don't know why that is, but I've seen it happen over and over again."

"It's harder to be diligent than it is to be brave," said Mrs. Wogus. "That's why. You can be brave for two seconds and then it's all over. But to be diligent takes anywhere from a month to ten years."

"I guess maybe that's it," said Adoniram.

"Well, it's too bad. I do want to find Byram, on Georgie's account as well as my own."

"Now, don't you be discouraged," said Mrs. Wiggins. "My land, these animals may not care such a lot about working for the medal, but as soon as they know about how you feel they'll work their heads off to find that boy. Here, you stop fretting about it and leave it to me."

When Mrs. Wiggins said something would happen, it pretty generally happened. She was big and clumsy, and she made more mistakes than you would believe one cow could make, but when anybody was in trouble he always came to Mrs. Wiggins, rather than her partner in the detective business, the brilliant but erratic Freddy, who was as likely as not to stop in the middle of tracking down a criminal case and start writing poetry or drawing plans for a new pigpen or doing any one of the thousand things to which he could turn his hand.

And so the next day Mrs. Wiggins said to her sisters: "I'm going out to take a walk. I want to think about this boy." She always went out for a walk when anything was bothering her, because she said she thought better when she was walking.

But the real reason was that she couldn't think at home, because her sisters talked all the time. And then of course she'd get to talking with them, and her thinking just wouldn't get done. Very few people can talk and think at the same time, even on the same subject.

Mrs. Wiggins walked down past the pond, and waved a hoof at Alice and Emma, but went on without speaking. The two ducks looked at each other.

"Something on her mind," said Alice. "She isn't usually so formal."

"I wonder what it is," said Emma. "I supposed everything was all right, now that Adoniram has been adopted. Dear, dear, I hope there isn't any more trouble."

"Let's ask her," said Alice.

So the two ducks swam ashore and waddled, quacking anxiously, after the cow. Pretty soon Mrs. Wiggins heard them and turned around.

"What is it, girls?" she asked. She always called them girls, because she knew it pleased them, although they had a dozen grand-nephews and nieces on the farm.

"Is—is anything the matter, dear Mrs. Wiggins," asked Emma. "We thought you looked worried."

"Good gracious, no," said the cow with her deep hearty laugh. "I was just trying to think of some way of finding where that boy Byram is living." And she told them of her talk with Adoniram. "He wants a real playmate, a real boy. Bertram's all very well, but, after all, he's really nothing but a rooster."

"Deary me," said Emma, "I do wish Uncle Wesley were here. His advice was always so sound. I'm sure he would have known just what to do."

"I'm sure he would," said Mrs. Wiggins, hiding a smile. It is hard for a cow to hide a smile, because she has such a large face, but Mrs. Wiggins did it. She did it by stepping behind a tree for a minute. She remembered the ducks' Uncle Wesley well enough. He was a fat, pompous little duck who had tyrannized over his female relatives until the farm animals, who were fond of Alice and Emma, had kidnapped him one night and turned him over to an eagle, who for a small consideration had carried him off into the next county. Uncle Wesley had never come back, and

Alice and Emma were at last able to call their souls their own. But they still revered his memory.

"But I should think the circus man could help you," said Alice. "He's an awfully nice man, and he travels all over the country."

"My goodness," said Mrs. Wiggins, "Mr. Boomschmidt! Of course—he's just the person. Now, why didn't I think of that?"

"You probably would have in a minute," said Emma politely.

"Well, we'll never know," said the cow. "Anyway, I'm going to walk right over to the Centerboro fair grounds and see him. Freddy had a postcard from some of the circus animals yesterday saying they would get into Centerboro some time today. They give a show there tomorrow, and a lot of us were talking about going over." And she thanked the ducks and trotted off.

The Boomschmidt circus came to Centerboro to give its performance twice every summer, and the animals on the Bean farm had got quite well acquainted with the circus animals. Two years before, Freddy had done some detective work for them helping to solve an extremely difficult case, and they were all pretty grateful. Mrs. Wiggins knew that they would help her if they possibly could.

On the way through the barnyard she found Adoniram and Bertram shooting marbles. "Hop up on my back, Adoniram," she said. "We're going over to Centerboro to see the circus come in."

Adoniram had been hoping that someone would ask him to go over. He was going to the circus next day, of course, but it is almost as much fun to see the wagons come in, and watch the tents put up, and talk to the animals beforehand, as it is to see the performance. So he jumped on Mrs. Wiggins's back and they set off.

When they got to the fair grounds the big tent was already up, but the side-show tents were still spread out on the ground, and men were hammering pegs, and elephants and tigers and camels and animals of all kinds were hurrying about as busy as ants in a thunderstorm, and all was bustle and confusion.

"Hello, Mrs. Wiggins," said a voice, and a small and very nice-looking brown bear came up to them.

"Why, Freginald," said the cow, "well, you're

looking fine! How are you? Shake hands with my friend, Adoniram R. Bean."

The bear held out a paw. Adoniram shook it.

"Where's Mr. Boomschmidt?" asked Mrs. Wiggins. "We want to ask his advice about something."

"I'll find him for you," said Freginald. "Hi, Leo," he called to a lion who was lying down in the shadow of a wagon, "where's the chief?"

The lion, whose mane was beautifully curled and arranged in a sort of swirl at the back of the head, said without opening his eyes: "In the big tent." Then his eyes opened, he blinked twice, and jumped to his feet. "Well, dye my hair!" he said. "If it isn't Mrs. Wiggins! How are you? And your charming sisters? I was just saying to Mr. Boomschmidt—'Chief,' I said, 'if Mrs. Wiggins isn't in the front row tomorrow, I won't do my act. I won't come on,' I said."

"Get along with you!" said Mrs. Wiggins, looking pleased. "They couldn't keep you away from an audience if they locked you in a cage." Then she introduced Adoniram, who was quite excited at meeting a real lion, and they went into the big tent.

Over in the far corner of the tent a crowd of animals and men were standing in a circle, watching a mud-turtle who was climbing up a rope. "Another amateur," Leo explained, "who wants to get a job."

As they came closer, a small round man in a bright-checked suit, with his hat pushed far on the back of his head, picked the turtle off the rope and set him on the ground. "All right," he said. "That'll do. My gracious, that's a good trick, all right. But it won't do for our audiences. Eh, Leo?" he said, catching sight of the lion. "Tell him why it won't do for our audiences."

"Quite right, chief," said Leo. "He's a turtle, and he can climb a rope. So what? What does he do when he has climbed it? Nothing. Well, you can't ask an audience to look at that."

"That's it," said Mr. Boomschmidt. "That's it exactly. See here, my boy," he said to the turtle, "you go home and think up something to do. Then practice it. And come see me next year."

"But what shall I do when I've climbed the rope, sir?" asked the turtle.

"Oh, dear me! Oh, my goodness!" exclaimed Mr. Boomschmidt. "How should I know?

You're the one to do it—not me. Think of something—a high dive, a juggling act, anything. Now run along. Sorry." Then he turned around. "Well, as I live and breathe!" he exclaimed. "Mrs. Wiggins!" And he rushed over and held out his hand. "How are you, and the good Beans, and Jinx, and that clever pig—what's his name? Now, why can't I think of it? Gracious me, why can't I ever remember names? I'd know his face anywhere, but his name—Leo, what is that pig's name?"

"Freddy," said the lion.

"Freddy! Of course. Handsome fellow, too. Well, well, it's a pleasure to see you."

When Mrs. Wiggins had finally explained about Byram, and how they had been unable to get any information about him, Mr. Boomschmidt said: "Well, well, I guess we'll have to go into conference about this."

"Where's that?" said Mrs. Wiggins.

"Oh, dear me, it isn't a place; it's a state. Like— What is it like, Leo?"

"Like being in love," said the lion. "Or in difficulties. Or—"

"Now you're just being confusing," said Mr.

159

Boomschmidt. "Good grief, being in love and being in difficulties—why they're entirely different."

"Not entirely," said Leo. "But, chief, I was just illustrating—"

"Well, you're not supposed to illustrate—not when you're in conference. Now I call the conference to order. Anybody got any suggestions? No? Then what game'll we play?"

"But, Mr. Boomschmidt," protested Mrs. Wiggins, "we can't play games—not now. I thought maybe you could help us find this Byram boy."

"Dear, dear, so you did," said Mr. Boomschmidt. "I'm sorry. It was being in conference that got me mixed up. We always play games in conference. Well, Leo, speak up, what'll we do about Byram? Offer a reward? Advertise?"

"I should think that would be a good idea," said Freginald. "We could put up a notice offering a reward for information leading to the discovery of the whereabouts of a boy, such and such an age, such and such a name—"

"Why bring in his whereabouts?" said Mr. Boomschmidt. "We don't want his whereabouts; we want the boy. And why say such and such? Why not *give* his name? What is his name, by the way?"

"Byram R. Jones."

"Jones," said Mr. Boomschmidt, "I've heard that name somewhere. And what does the R. stand for?"

"We don't know."

"Like the D. in John D. Rockefeller," said Leo. "Nobody knows what that stands for either, I bet."

The conference went on like this for some time, and it all seemed pretty confusing to Adoniram. He was surprised to find that when it was over, something had really been done. Since Georgie had said that he looked so much like Byram, it was decided to use his picture on the handbill that was drawn up, and a photographer was brought in to take it. Mr. Boomschmidt said he would have the bills distributed to everyone who came to the circus, and Leo and Freginald agreed to speak to all the animals. "And if we don't find him before the summer's over," said Mr. Boomschmidt, "I miss my guess."

Adoniram and Mrs. Wiggins spent the rest of the day at the fair grounds, wandering around and chatting with the animals and seeing how the circus was run. And when they went home, Mr. Boomschmidt gave them each a free pass for the show next day.

Neither of them said much on their way back to the farm. But all at once Mrs. Wiggins began to chuckle. "That Leo," she said. "He tickles me."

"I thought he was awfully nice," said Adoniram.

"He is nice," said the cow. "But that mane of his—did you see how he had it arranged? They say he spends half his time looking at pictures in women's magazines of new ways to do your hair. He gets a permanent wave twice a year, and he's always running to beauty shops. I bet you that hair-do he had was the latest thing from Paris." They walked a way in silence, then she began to chuckle again. "Him and his permanents," she said. "Him and his permanents!"

x Bertram Wrestles at the Circus

Mr. Boomschmidt and his partner, Mr. Hackenmeyer, didn't believe that animals should be shut up in cages. And so their circus was quite different from most circuses. The lions and tigers and bears and elephants and camels and all the other animals walked around among the people and chatted with them and cracked jokes and gave little boys rides, and often after the show started they would sit with friends in the audience until their act came on. It was all very friendly and nice. Of course people who had never been to this show before were sometimes scared, and you can't really blame them, for it is a little terrifying to walk into the circus grounds and come face to face with a Bengal tiger, or to be tapped on the shoulder and turn around to have a boa constrictor say: "May I show you to a seat?" But Adoniram thought it was wonderful.

The animals from the Bean farm had come in a body, led by the phaeton, in which sat Mr. and Mrs. Bean and Uncle Ben and Adoniram and Bertram. After they had walked around for a while and renewed old friendships, and visited some of the side shows, they filed into the big tent to take the two rows of seats which had been reserved for them opposite the band. There was a burst of applause as they sat down, for they were quite famous in Centerboro. And then there was a roar of laughter. For Mr. Bean had risen to take a bow, and when he took off his old felt hat everybody saw that under it he still had on his white nightcap with the red tassel. He had been so excited about going to the circus that he had forgotten to take it off when he got up.

Mrs. Bean's face turned red and she jumped up and snatched off the nightcap, and Mr. Bean looked puzzled for a minute and then laughed and waved his hand. And everybody clapped. And then the show began.

I'm not going to tell you about the show. Maybe you'll go some day and see it for yourself, and I hope you'll enjoy it as much as Adoniram did. Mr. Bean bought peanuts and popcorn for all the animals, and they sat and munched and watched and applauded. Bertram didn't applaud, because Ronald found that he couldn't see everything that was going on through the little window in the clockwork boy's chest, so he left the control room and came outside. He went back in once, though. That was when twenty-five roosters came out dressed up in red uniforms and did some fancy marching. Ronald scrambled back into the control room and made Bertram clap his hands until the splinters flew from them.

Adoniram saw a lot of the audience looking at the handbills offering a reward for Byram, which had been handed them as they bought their tickets. And a good many of them kept looking at him, too, and then whispering to their neighbors. And just before the show was over, quite a number got up and went out. Adoniram didn't think anything about it then, but when the band played the final number and everybody started to go, he heard a commotion outside, and as he came out through the tent door, a big shout went up. "There he is!—I claim the reward!—That's the boy!"

The rush of the crowd toward him shoved him back inside the tent. As he and the animals were pushed back, he saw Mr. Boomschmidt standing up in the little ticket-seller's pulpit at the entrance, waving his arms and shouting over and over: "Ladies and gentlemen! Ladies and gentlemen!" But nobody listened to him.

Adoniram saw right away what had happened. The people had seen his picture on the handbill and had naturally jumped to the conclusion that he was Byram. For the bill had said: "Have you seen Byram R. Jones? This is what he looks like." It hadn't said that the picture was a picture of Adoniram.

As the boy was wondering what to do, Leo appeared from somewhere. "Come on," he said. "We'll get out the back way. If you go out there now, they'll all try to grab you and claim the reward, and they'll get to fighting over you and tear you to pieces. The chief'll calm 'em down as soon as they'll let him speak. He'll explain about that handbill."

"Maybe I could speak to them," said Bertram. "I could make them hear." And Ronald turned up the microphone and shouted: "Ladies and Gentlemen!" in Bertram's loudest voice.

"Well, dye my hair!" exclaimed Leo looking at him admiringly. "A natural baritone with all the power of a steamboat whistle! Sure, go out and explain."

So Bertram went out and got up beside Mr. Boomschmidt, and when that big voice rolled out across the crowd there was instant silence. So Bertram explained that the picture on the bill was not a picture of the missing boy, but of a boy who looked like him and who was thought to be his brother.

There was a good deal of grumbling, and one man shouted: "Well, who are you, then? You look just like him, too."

So Bertram explained who he was, and why he had been painted to look like Adoniram, and then he showed some of the things he could do. Nearly everybody was satisfied with that, and they laughed and applauded when he did his tricks. But the man who had spoken before said: "Yah! You're no more clockwork than my boy here. There's some trickery, folks. I believe this is the missing boy, and I claim the reward."

And the man's son, who was bigger than Bertram, came up close to the ticket booth and made a face and said: "Yah! Want to fight?"

"No," said Bertram, "I don't want to fight. I just want to tell you—"

"Yah!" said the boy again. "Don't want to fight, hey? Want to rassle?"

"No," said Bertram, "I don't want to rassle. I just want to—"

"Yah, yah, yah!" said the boy, making still worse faces. "Scaredy-cat!"

"That's the stuff, Benjy," said the man. "If we can't get the reward, let's have some fun. Rassle him— Hey, what's this?" he shouted. For something like a thick rope had snapped around his waist, and he turned to look up into the calm eyes of old Hannibal, the elephant. And at the same moment, Louise, a smaller elephant, had grabbed the boy. Mr. Boomschmidt had slipped away and brought them back.

"My goodness," said Mr. Boomschmidt, "I don't want to put you off the grounds, but this is a circus, not a battlefield. If you want to rassle, why, rassle these elephants."

"You put me down," roared the boy. "You big coward," he shouted to Bertram.

Adoniram had come out, and now he said to Mr. Boomschmidt: "We can't let him call Bertram names in front of everybody. But we can't let him wrestle Bertram, either. He wouldn't have a show. Let me wrestle him."

"You're smaller than he is," said Mr. Boomschmidt doubtfully.

"Yes, but Bertram and I have wrestled a lot together, and Peter, the bear, has taught me a lot about wrestling, too."

But the boy didn't want to wrestle with Adoniram. "I'm not going to fight with anybody who's been taught by a bear," he said. "Anyway, it's that one I dared to rassle." And he pointed to Bertram. "If he dassent, let him say so."

"All right," said Bertram at last. "Put him down, Louise. I'll rassle him."

So the people formed a ring about them, and Louise put Benjy down. Benjy took off his coat and crouched down as Bertram walked up to him with his arms spread wide apart. "Now I'll show you something," said Benjy, and he leaped at Bertram and threw his arms around Bertram's neck and twisted.

Well, he might as well have tried to wrestle with a telephone pole. Bertram just stood and let him work for a while, then his arms came together around Benjy's waist and he lifted him right off the ground. Benjy yelled and grabbed Bertram's nose and tried to twist that, but Bertram didn't pay any attention. He shifted his grip until he had the struggling boy under one arm, then he went over and sat down with his back against a tree. "Guess I'll take a little nap," he said. And his head nodded and his eyelids clicked shut and he began to snore gently.

Benjy wriggled and struck out, but the more he struggled, the tighter Bertram held him and the louder he snored. And everybody began to laugh. Everybody, that is, except Benjy's father. He came forward and grabbed Bertram by the shoulder and said: "Hey, you; that isn't wrestling. You don't fight fair. Let the boy up."

Bertram's arm loosened and Benjy got free.

"He didn't throw you," said the man. "He didn't get you down. Now go in and let's see you put him on his back."

"I will not," said Benjy. "I've had enough. I ain't going to fight with no piece of furniture."

"Well, I will, then," said the man. And he took off his hat and jumped on it, and he threw off his coat and dove at Bertram.

Bertram didn't even bother to wake up. The man was big and strong, and he tugged and heaved and tried hold after hold, but Bertram had a good firm grip of a tent peg with one hand, and the man couldn't even turn him over. The more people laughed, the madder the man got. And at last he got up and jumped on Bertram.

"Here, here," said Mr. Boomschmidt, "that's no way to rassle. Hannibal, pull him off."

But Ronald didn't like the jumping either, for he was afraid that something might get broken. And before Hannibal could reach them, he grabbed the man by the leg, pulled him down, and fell on him.

The man just went "Whoosh!" and didn't move. Bertram wasn't very big, but he must have weighed two hundred and fifty pounds with all the machinery in him. He didn't move either.

"Have you had enough?" he said.

The man growled and grumbled for a little, but he had no breath left, and at last he said crossly: "Yes." So Bertram got up and helped him to his feet and brushed him off, and then held out his hand. But the man wouldn't take it. He seized Benjy by the arm and dragged him off through the crowd. He was never seen around Centerboro again.

This wrestling match created a lot of talk around Centerboro and people came out to the farm to see the clockwork boy, and then the New York papers got hold of it and sent photographers to take Bertram's picture and reporters to ask him how he liked the United States and what his favorite color was and things like that. Mr. Bean got pretty cross about people picnicking on his lawn, and knocking at the door at all hours of the day and night, and sneaking along behind fences and pointing cameras at him. So the animals got Peter, the bear, to patrol the barnyard, and they put Sniffy Wilson on the gate to scare away reporters and sightseers. They weren't bothered much after that.

But one thing all the stories in the papers did—they brought the reward for Byram to the attention of every man, woman, and child in the country. And two weeks after the circus left Centerboro, a big package came by express for Freddy from Mr. Boomschmidt. It contained nearly three hundred letters from people in every state in the union, claiming that they knew where Byram was and asking for the reward.

Freddy took them to Adoniram. "I expect you and Georgie, as the people most concerned, ought to go through these," he said. "Most of them are probably either fakes or cases of mistaken identity, but you can pick out those that look the best and I'll investigate them."

"Here's one from Cuba," said Adoniram. "It isn't very likely that Byram would have got down there."

"No," said the pig. "I think we'd better investigate the near-by ones first."

So they sorted the letters by states, and then Adoniram read the New York ones out loud to Georgie, who had never learned to read, and they picked out six and took them to Freddy.

Freddy looked thoughtful. "H'm," he said.

"One from Batavia, two from Binghamton —here, here's one from Dutch Flats. That's just down the river a way. Then—Lockport, Jordan, Rome. And Byram may not be in any of these places. Well, Adoniram, if we go through these, and then Ohio and Pennsylvania, Byram will be an old man with long gray whiskers before we find him. Still, there's one thing that strikes me. Most of the New York towns are on the canal. Looks as if maybe some of these people really have seen him if he's traveling along the canal."

"Maybe he's living on a canal boat," said Georgie. "That's where most of the letters say they saw him."

"All except the one from Dutch Flats," said Adoniram. "That says there's a boy that looks like the picture in the big orphanage down there."

"We'll take that first," said the pig. "Georgie and I will go down there this afternoon. Then if we don't find him, I've got an idea how we can get to work on the other letters without too much trouble."

XI   *Freddy* B*ecomes a* T*rustee*

Freddy did most of his detective work in disguise. He had a great many different costumes hanging up in his study, and whole drawers full of wigs and false beards and dark spectacles and various other things to use in changing his appearance. He usually had a good deal of trouble with the disguises. Most of the clothing was much too big for him and he was always tripping over it and getting tangled up in it, and sometimes parts of the disguise would fall off, disclosing him for what he was. Not that there was ever much doubt, for he always looked a good deal like a pig, whatever he put on. The other animals wondered why he used the disguises at all, but he always said it was a lot more fun to do it that way. And perhaps that is as good a reason for doing anything as you can find.

Today he was disguised as an old woman. He had on an old gingham dress of Mrs. Bean's, and a big sunbonnet from under which two long corkscrew curls hung down on his shoulders, and he had pulled on a pair of black lace mitts over his fore trotters. The dress was too long for him, and he had torn off part of the front, leaving the back to drag behind him like a train. On his arm he had a shopping bag with a picture of the Bridge of Sighs on it. As Jinx said when he saw him, if you didn't guess who he was right off, you might think he was something human, or you might decide not to take any chances and run up a tree.

As they walked along the dusty road, Freddy kept twisting around to try to see how he looked. This is almost impossible anyway unless you have a mirror, and if you are a medium-sized pig with your head concealed in a bonnet as big as a bushel basket, it is entirely impossible. Freddy just kept switching his train around and kicking up dust, and finally after Georgie had sneezed about twenty times, he said:

"Say, look, Freddy. We've got a long way to go, and maybe you can get there in that rig, but if I swallow any more dust you'll have to carry me too. Why can't you take it off?"

So Freddy reluctantly took off the disguise and rolled it up and slung it around his neck. He put it on again before they got to Dutch Flats a couple of hours later. He was just tying the strings of the sunbonnet when a boy on a bicycle came up behind them and stopped and said: "Excuse me, ma'am, is this glove yours? I found it back there in the road." And he held out one of the lace mitts.

"Dear me," said Freddy taking the mitt, "how could I have been so careless! I wouldn't have lost one of them for anything—they were a gift from my dear husband. Thank you, my little man. Here is a penny for you." And he fumbled in the shopping bag, and then said: "Dear me, I don't seem to have any pennies."

"Oh, that's all right, ma'am," said the boy. He said it rather indistinctly, for he was holding his hand over his mouth and evidently trying not to laugh.

"What is the matter with you, boy?" said Freddy severely.

At that the boy burst out in a loud and uncontrollable laugh. "Oh, please excuse me," he said. "I—it was just so funny to think of a pig having any pennies."

"A pig?"

"Sure. I saw you were a pig right away. But I thought you didn't want me to notice it, and I did try not to, really I did. You're that detective from over Centerboro way, aren't you?"

"Bah!" said Freddy crossly, and turned his back and walked off.

Georgie winked at the boy and followed his friend. Neither of them said anything until they got to the orphanage. It was a long low white building, and fifteen or twenty boys were playing games on the wide green lawn in front. They didn't pay much attention as the two animals went up the walk to the front door, and Georgie said: "They're pretty polite boys."

"Too polite," said the pig. "Somebody must be watching them from a window."

And sure enough, before Freddy could ring the bell, the door opened and a severe-looking woman in a sort of nurse's uniform stood looking down on them.

"How do you do?" said Freddy. "Is the matron in?"

"Have an appointment with her?" asked the woman.

"Oh yes," said Freddy. "She's expecting me."

Now, the matron was having tea that afternoon with the trustees of the orphanage, and so the severe-looking woman, whose name was Miss Winch, thought that Freddy was a trustee too. And she couldn't see him very well because he was standing against the bright outdoor light. So she said: "Well, I guess you can go right in," and stood aside.

"Thank you," said Freddy, and started in with Georgie after him.

"You can't take that dog in," said the woman. "Miss Threep doesn't like dogs."

"Dear me," said Freddy, "why I never go anywhere without my dear little Georgie. Still, of course, rules are rules, aren't they?" He leaned down and patted Georgie kindly on the head.

"There, Georgie, you run along and play with the nice little boys. Maybe you'll see somebody you know. And please be a good little doggy. Mamma'll be out pretty soon."

"Mamma'd better watch her step or she'll be thrown out," growled Georgie under his breath.

Freddy of course didn't know anything about the tea-party, and he was horrified when he went through the door which Miss Winch opened for him and found himself in a big room full of people. But he couldn't back out. He edged around into a dim corner of the room, hoping that nobody would notice him. And for a few minutes nobody did. But then, one by one, the people who were sitting and standing about, drinking tea and nibbling sandwiches and talking, caught sight of him. And one by one they stopped drinking and nibbling and talking and just stared. And at last Miss Threep saw him.

Miss Threep was almost as severe-looking as Miss Winch, and indeed she could be pretty severe when she had to, but all the boys in the orphanage liked her because she was fair about things, and she didn't see why boys shouldn't have a good time just because they were orphans.

She had a nice smile, and she smiled it now as she went up to Freddy and held out her hand and said: "You're Mrs. Winfield Church, aren't you?"

"Yes," said Freddy, because he didn't know what else to say, and he shook hands with her.

"Goodness, your hands are cold," exclaimed Miss Threep. "Come have some tea."

"No, thank you," said Freddy. "Couldn't we —just sit here?"

"Of course," said Miss Threep, and they sat down.

Now, the most important of all the trustees, and the richest, was Mrs. Winfield Church, but neither Miss Threep nor any of the other trustees had ever seen her because she lived in France. But she had come back to America that spring and had written Miss Threep that she would come to the tea-party.

"Well, well," said Miss Threep, "I am certainly glad to make your acquaintance at last, Mrs. Church. How courageous of you to leave Paris in the spring! And I do want to show you over the building. I want you to see for yourself how things are run. And I hope you will let me

introduce the other trustees to you, for they are all very anxious to meet you. But first perhaps there are some questions you'd like to ask."

"Well," thought Freddy, "I have got by so far, and maybe Miss Threep thinks this sunbonnet and gingham dress are the latest thing from Paris. Anyway, she doesn't act as if she thought I looked funny." And as the other people had politely gone back to their tea and conversation, he began to feel better.

"Well," he said, "there is one thing I'd like to ask. It is about a boy named Byram Jones, who I understand—"

But he never got any further, for at that moment the door flew open and a large woman all covered with pearls and diamonds and other jewels sailed into the room and said: "I am afraid I am very late. I am Mrs. Winfield Church."

Miss Threep jumped up as if a pin had been stuck into her and said: "What! But this lady here has just told me that *she* is Mrs. Winfield Church."

And everybody came up and crowded around Freddy.

Freddy was pretty scared. But there's one

thing about a pig—he seldom loses his head. "Dear me," he said, "your name really is Mrs. Winfield Church? How odd that there should be two of us of the same name here today."

"Very odd," said Mrs. Church dryly, and some of the trustees looked at Freddy's dilapidated clothes and compared them with Mrs. Church's rich garments, and then they snickered. But being trustees, they tried to do it as politely as possible, for trustees are not supposed to laugh out loud.

"Well," said the head trustee, "I suppose it is possible. But as you are not a trustee of this orphanage, and as this lady is certainly *the* Mrs. Winfield Church, I suggest, madam, that you leave. I think you have made a mistake. You are probably looking for the poorhouse, which is about half a mile down this road."

Now, Freddy was a good actor and if he hadn't looked so much like a pig, could have made his fortune on the stage. Indeed, when the animals put on shows, as they sometimes did, Freddy was always given the leading part, and his Hamlet was something to see. The secret of his success was that not only did he act like the person he was supposed to be, he felt like that person. He forgot that he was a pig and he *was* that person. And so now he was a little old woman in shabby clothing who had been insulted by a fat man with a heavy gold watch-chain. He stared at the head trustee for a minute, and then he said: "And why do you think I am looking for the poorhouse? Is it because my clothes are old and worn?"

"Oh, I'm sure Mr. Waldemar didn't mean that," said Miss Threep kindly.

"But I did," said the head trustee. "I'm a plain blunt man, and I say what I think."

"Then you think a lot of foolish things," said Freddy angrily. "There may be several reasons why my clothes are queer. Just as there may be several reasons why you are so fat. I may think it is because you eat too much. But I wouldn't say so unless I knew. Just because you have a gold watch-chain I wouldn't say that you stole it unless I was pretty certain. Just because—"

"That's enough of this," said the head trustee, swelling up and turning dark red. "Miss Threep, either this woman leaves the room or I do."

"Wait a minute," said Mrs. Winfield Church suddenly, and everybody including Mr. Waldemar looked at her respectfully. She seemed to be smiling to herself, and Freddy thought that under all the diamonds and pearls and ribbons she had on she looked a lot like Mrs. Wiggins. "I have always thought," said Mrs. Church, "that trustees' meetings and tea-parties were pretty dull affairs, and that is why I have stayed in Paris so long—so I wouldn't have to attend them. I find this one, however, is anything but dull. And in order to keep it from getting dull, I suggest that this lady, who seems to be my namesake, be asked to stay."

There was a general murmur of assent, through which Mr. Waldemar's voice said: "But she is not a trustee."

"What of it?" said Mrs. Church. "This isn't a secret meeting, is it? We're not going to have any of the boys executed, are we?"

"I shall leave," said the head trustee pompously. "I do not propose—"

"Oh, go on—leave then," interrupted Mrs. Church. And she turned away from him and went to the piano and began to play a dance. And pretty soon all the trustees were dancing together. But Mr. Waldemar sat in the corner and tried to look like a plain blunt man who disapproved of such goings on.

Well, Miss Threep sent for fresh tea and more sandwiches, and they played charades and had a fine time generally. Freddy sang several songs of his own composition and Mrs. Church accompanied him. And finally Mr. Waldemar got up and came out of his corner and said he'd like to sing. So he sang *Asleep in the Deep* in a fine bass voice, and everybody applauded, even the boys out in the playground. And Mr. Waldemar was so gratified that he came over and apologized to Freddy, and Freddy sang a duet with him.

But all this time Freddy hadn't given a moment's thought to what he had come there for, and it wasn't until the party began to break up that it occurred to him that he ought to ask about Byram. He went up to Miss Threep, who was talking with Mrs. Church by the piano, and said: "Excuse me, Miss Threep, but there was something I wanted to ask you—"

"Just a minute," put in Mrs. Church. "You get your hat on, Miss Threep. I am going to take this lady home, and you come along for the ride, and she can ask you what she wants to know."

So Miss Threep got her hat and they went out and got into a huge black shiny car that was almost as long as Mr. Bean's barn. As Freddy was getting in, Georgie ran up. "Oh," said Freddy, "here is my Georgie. Could you take him too, Mrs. Church?"

Mrs. Church said she could, so Georgie jumped in beside the chauffeur.

"That's my little man," said Freddy, leaning forward from where he sat between the two ladies and patting the dog on the head. "Was he a good little doggy today? And did he miss his mamma?"

"He's a nice little dog," said Miss Threep.

"He means well," said Freddy, "and he's very affectionate, but he's not very bright." He was going on to say more, but Georgie gave him such a grim look that he decided not to.

"Well," said Miss Threep, "what was it you wanted to see me about?"

"I wanted to ask you about a boy who, I was told, is in the orphanage," said Freddy. "But first—you've been so nice to me I think I ought to tell you—my name isn't Mrs. Winfield Church."

"How could it be?" said Mrs. Church easily.

"I mean, I'm—I'm not a lady. I'm—well, I'm a pig."

"Dear me," said Miss Threep. "I don't think you ought to feel that way."

"No," said Freddy, "I don't mean that. I mean I really am a pig."

"Of course he's a pig," said Mrs. Church. "I saw that almost from the first. Yes, and I think I know who you are, too. I saw a piece about you in the Paris *Herald* awhile ago." And she began to laugh.

"Good heavens!" exclaimed Miss Threep. "A pig! Of course I'm rather nearsighted, but those curls—"

"Pinned in the sunbonnet," said Freddy. "See?" and he took the bonnet off.

"Well, I declare," said Miss Threep. "You fooled me completely."

"It's about the first time I ever did, then," said Freddy. "But perhaps I'd better tell you the whole story." And so he did.

"I'm afraid I can't help you much," said Miss Threep when he had finished. "We had a boy named Byram in the orphanage for about a month. And he had been traveling along the canal. But he ran away again three weeks ago, and we haven't been able to find him. He was a nice boy, too. But why did you disguise yourself to come ask me about him? I'd have told you what I know anyway."

"Well, I thought he might be in the orphanage, and if he was, I was going to try to adopt him. And I knew you wouldn't let a pig adopt a boy."

"No," said Miss Threep thoughtfully. "I suppose the trustees wouldn't have approved. We've never had any applications like that. Well, I'll let you know if we hear any more about him. Then your Mr. Bean can apply for him. But I'm afraid we won't see him again. That boy is a traveler, and he is pretty well able to take care of himself, too. But one thing I can tell you. Hunt along the canal east of here. He was going toward Albany, and that's where you are most likely to find him."

The big car had turned in at the Beans' gate by this time, and as it drew up in the barnyard, half a dozen animals came out to look it over.

"What a nice farm!" said Mrs. Church.

"Land's sakes, Freddy, is that you?" said Mrs. Bean, coming to the door. "Won't you ask your friends in?"

So the two ladies got out and met Mrs. Bean and Adoniram. "Well, I never!" said Mrs. Bean, when she heard about Freddy's visit to the orphanage. "What won't these animals be up to next! They're nice animals, all of 'em, and as good as gold, but there's never a dull moment on this farm. But won't you ladies stay to supper? I know Mr. Bean'd be as pleased as Punch."

So they stayed to supper, and afterwards Adoniram and Freddy took them out and introduced them to all the other animals, and to Uncle Ben and Bertram. Uncle Ben gave each of them one of his new firecracker alarm clocks, and they were much pleased with them. Miss Threep had to be back at the orphanage by nine o'clock, but Mrs. Church was so delighted with everything that when it was time for them to start she hadn't yet got back to the car. She was down in the cow barn, where she had struck up a great friendship with Mrs. Wiggins; and the others, waiting by the car, could hear their laughter. But at last she came.

"Goodness," she said, "I haven't laughed so in years. I'm coming out here again. That Mrs. Wiggins! Why, she's as like my sister Eva as two peas."

"It's a wonderful place for Adoniram," said Miss Threep. "I wish my boys at the orphanage had a lot of nice animals to play with."

"Good land, bring 'em out any time," said Mrs. Bean. "There's plenty of animals here, and they like boys. Glad to have 'em."

"I'll send them over in my car any time, Miss Threep," said Mrs. Church.

When they had gone, Freddy went down to his study and brushed and hung up his costume, and then threw himself down in his big chair. But he jumped up again with a squeal, for several large stones had been shoved in under the cover of the cushion. As he stood rubbing himself, he heard a faint giggle, and he made a dive under the table and pulled out Georgie.

"Hello, mamma," said Georgie, struggling to get away. "How's my mamma? Did she hurt herself on the nassy old chair?"

"You—you pup!" said Freddy. "Playing tricks on me, are you?"

"Oh, no, mamma!" said Georgie. "I was just trying to make my mamma's chair nice and comfortable, but I'm not very bright, and maybe I did it wrong. Did I, mamma, huh?"

Freddy scowled at him, then he laughed and let him go. "Well, I guess we're even," he said. "But now get out of here. I'm going to bed."

"Kiss Georgie good-night?" said the dog, then turned and dashed through the door, and heard the bolt snap into place behind him.

XII *The Expedition Sets Out*

The four mice—Eek and Quik and Eeny and Cousin Augustus—were sitting on the end of a beam that stuck out under the gable of the barn. It was the first really hot day of summer, but up there there was always a little breeze. Eek and Eeny were talking about things they liked to eat, and Cousin Augustus was asleep as usual, and Quik had a toothache, so that he was pretty quiet. Only now and then he would say: "Ouch!" so that the others wouldn't forget his tooth, or to feel sorry for him.

At first they had felt sorry for him. But after

he had said: "Ouch!" about two hundred times they didn't have any sorry feeling left.

"I wish you'd shut up about that tooth," said Eeny finally. "All you have to do is have it out, and then it won't ache any more."

"That's all you know about it," said Quik. "And I must say you aren't very sympathetic. When I'm suffering tortures! Oh! Ouch! There it goes again."

Cousin Augustus opened one eye, stretched, opened the other eye, and gave a loud yawn. At least it was loud for a mouse. "Still yawping about that tooth?" he inquired sleepily. "Go on in and see Uncle Ben. He'll yank it out with those little pliers of his. Just one terrible final pang, and it's gone forever. Whew, I'm *hot!* And sticky. Wonder why it always makes you sticky to sleep in the daytime? Let's go down and have a swim."

Quik followed his brothers slowly down from the beam. They had to pass through the loft where Uncle Ben was at work on his clocks. Suddenly Eek and Eeny, who had been whispering together, turned and grabbed Quik and they dragged him, protesting shrilly, up on to the work-bench. Then Cousin Augustus held his mouth open with his paws.

"Tooth?" said Uncle Ben.

"Yes, he's decided to have it out at last," said Eeny.

Quik tried to say something, but both Cousin Augustus's forepaws were in his mouth so all that came out was a faint squeak.

Uncle Ben didn't use his pliers. He just reached in with a finger and thumb and the tooth was so loose that it almost fell into his hand. Then he scratched the still struggling Quik gently between the ears, grinned at him, and went back to his work.

Quik was pretty mad, and he said what he thought of his brothers in no uncertain terms. But pretty soon he calmed down. For after he had poked his tongue into the hole where the tooth had been a few times, he found that the ache was indeed gone. "Just the same," he said, "you didn't have to drag me in like that. I was going anyway. I just didn't like to—*erk!*" he went hiccuping suddenly. "There! You see? Now you've given me the hiccups."

They went down across the barnyard to the

duck pond. Alice and Emma were sitting comfortably under the shade of a bush, and Quik joined them while the other three mice plunged into the water.

"Why aren't you going in, Quik?" Alice asked.

"I just had my tooth pulled," said the mouse. "I was afraid I might catch cold in it."

Alice gave a little quacking laugh. "How funny you are, Quik! How could you catch cold in it if it isn't there?"

"He means that he might catch cold in the place where it was, sister," said Emma. "I don't think you ought to laugh at him. It must be dreadful to have teeth. You ought to be a duck, Quik."

"Erk!" said the mouse.

"I beg your pardon?" said Emma politely.

"I—that was just a hiccup. I didn't say anything."

"Oh, look, sister!" exclaimed Alice, ruffling her feathers in alarm. "Is that a hawk?"

High up in the blue above them a black speck was floating. It hardly seemed to move, then suddenly it began to grow in size—larger, larger, larger. . . .

Quacking distractedly, the ducks ran for cover, burrowing into the long grass. The mice were less frightened. There was little danger from a hawk they could see. It was only when a hawk pounced on them unawares that they might be caught. They crouched under the bank, watching.

The hawk came down like a bullet, his wings folded. But he was not aiming at the ducks. There was a tremendous splash in the middle of the pond, he went completely under, then came up, and they could hear the whistle of his feathers as his wings beat the air, and see the silvery gleam of the fish in his curved beak. He circled the pond, then lighted on a dead limb overhead.

He was a beautiful bird, almost as big as an eagle, with black and white plumage. He held the fish in one claw while he cocked his head to look down with fierce yellow eyes into the ducks' hiding-place.

"Come on out, girls," he said. "Today's Friday—fish day." He laughed and began to eat the fish. His laugh was harsh, but rather pleasant-sounding.

Alice and Emma came waddling out, smoothing down their feathers and trying to look dignified. "I guess we know an osprey when we see one," said Emma. "We weren't hiding. That is," she added, not wanting to be untruthful, "we weren't hiding from you."

"You'd be fools if you did," said the fish-hawk. "I'd have to be darned hungry to eat duck. No offence," he said quickly.

"None taken," said Alice. "But do you live around here? I haven't seen you before."

"Gosh, no, I come from up Boonville way. North of here a long ways. I'm just going down into the southern part of the state to visit my aunt. Not that I want to see her much. She's got pretty cranky the past few years, living alone as she does. But she lives on the Susquehanna, and I'm told that the fishing down there is pretty good this year, after the floods. Hope the fish are better than this one. Pretty brackish, he was. I expect this water is too stagnant."

"It's very good water," said Alice sharply. "It's the clearest, purest water in the county. My Uncle Wesley always said so, and he *knew*."

"Must be a terrible county," said the hawk, laughing again. "Oh now, don't get sore. I was only kidding you.—Well, what's the matter with that mouse?" For Quik, who with the other mice had come out on the bank, had hiccuped again.

"I've got the hiccups," said Quik. "I had a tooth pulled and that started me doing it, and now I can't stop."

"Do you want to stop?" asked the fish-hawk.

"Of course I want to stop," said Quik crossly. "You don't think I—erk!—enjoy it, do you?"

"Well, I dunno. I thought maybe you wanted to do it so you could give pleasure to others. It seems to amuse your friends."

"They aren't my friends, they're my brothers," said Quik.

"Ah, that's different," said the hawk seriously. "Well, I can stop the hiccups for you." He winked at the ducks, spread his wings, and rose in the air. He circled the pond once, then, with a quick swoop, swept up Quik in his strong claws, carried him out over the pond, and dropped him in.

Quik swam rapidly to shore. He stared up angrily at the hawk, who had returned to the dead limb. "You big bully," he said. "I'll get even with you for this. You wait—I'll—"

"Oh, come, come," said the hawk good-naturedly. "I didn't hurt you, did I? The only way to cure hiccups is to get good and scared. I scared 'em out of you. You ought to be grateful."

"Eh?" said Quik. "Why, you did. They're gone."

"Sure, they're gone. And I'd better be gone too, if I expect to get to my aunt's in time for dinner. Well, so long." With a swish of wings he took flight.

"Well, I must say," said Emma, "he's a lively one and no mistake. I wouldn't wonder if—"

"Here he comes back again," said Alice.

They looked up to see the hawk alight again on the dead branch.

"Say, look here," he said, "how'd that boy over there back of the pigpen get down here so quick?"

"Down here?" said Alice. "What do you mean? What boy?"

"He means Adoniram, I guess," said Eeny. "He's over there with Freddy, having a laughing lesson."

"Why, he lives here," said Alice.

"Go on," said the hawk. "I guess I know that

boy. I've seen him enough times lately, fishing in the canal up by Boonville. He was there when I left this morning, and unless he flew he couldn't have got here before I did."

"Wait a minute," said Cousin Augustus excitedly. "Do you know what he's saying, you people? A boy that looks like Adoniram, fishing in the canal? Oh, look, you, Mr. Whatever-your-name-is, where did you say that boy was?"

"Take it easy, mouse, or you'll be getting the hiccups like your brother," said the hawk. "What is all this, anyway?"

"Why, the boy you left this morning must be the boy we've all been looking for," said Alice. And she explained about the search for Byram. "But haven't you seen the notices in the papers, or the handbills Mr. Boomschmidt got out, offering a reward?"

"I'm not much of a hand for reading, and that's the truth," said the hawk. "But if what you say is so—"

"Certainly it is so," said Alice with dignity.

"All right, don't get het up. That's just a manner of speaking. I mean, if this is the boy, I can tell you where to find him all right. Whee! Boy, that's a classy car. Belong to your boss?"

A long black car had turned in at the gate, and they could see it bumping across the barnyard and down the lane to the pigpen, where it stopped. A chauffeur in a black uniform got out and opened the door, and a large woman, twinkling and fluttering all over with ribbons and jewels, was helped out. They saw her go forward, holding out her hand, and disappear on the other side of the pigpen.

"Some class," said the hawk. "We don't see 'em like that up around Boonville much. All rigged out like Washington crossing the Delaware, ain't she?"

"That's Mrs. Church," said Eek. "But look, would you go over and tell Freddy and Adoniram what you've just told us? And where to find this boy? You'll get the reward if he's the right one, you know."

"Don't give a cent for rewards," the hawk replied. "Lot of speeches, and a medal with about fifty cents' worth of silver in it. But I'm glad to be any help. Only I can't take all day. The Susquehanna's a-callin' me."

They hurried over to the pigpen, where they

found Freddy and Adoniram and Mrs. Church. Freddy had just told Mrs. Church about the laughing lessons, and some of the jokes that he used in them, and Mrs. Church was laughing so hard that for a few minutes they had to wait. When Mrs. Church laughed, she laughed all over, and as for conversation—you might as well have tried to talk in the middle of a band concert.

But pretty soon she stopped and wiped her eyes, and Alice went up to Adoniram and told him what they had just learned.

"The Black River Canal," said the boy. "Where's that?"

"It runs north from Rome," said the hawk.

"Rome is where one of those letters came from," said Freddy. "So Byram must have gone north instead of east. Well, I guess Georgie and I had better go up there and see if we can find him. You'd better come, too, Adoniram. How far is it?"

"About a hundred miles, I guess," said the hawk.

"H'm. It'll take us four or five days. Well, we can only hope he won't have gone on to some‚ where else by the time we get there."

"A hundred miles!" said Mrs. Church. "Why we can do it in three hours in my car. I'll take you. Get Georgie, Adoniram. And you animals hop in—yes, the mice too, if you'd like the ride. And the ducks."

Alice and Emma wanted to go, but they were a little terrified at the idea of traveling at high speed along the highway, and so they said politely: "Oh, thank you very much, but we really *think* . . . We don't want to crowd you."

Mrs. Church laughed. "If you think you two ducks can crowd *me*, just go ahead and try it. Come, hop in. There's plenty of room. Just move that alarm clock over, and keep it in the car to wake Riley up when it's time for him to call for me. I'd ask Mrs. Wiggins to go, but I'm afraid she couldn't manage the door. Now you"—she turned to the hawk—"tell the chauffeur just where to go."

So the hawk gave them directions, and said: "Oh, not at all, not at all; glad to be of service," when they thanked him. And as the big car, having stopped to pick up Georgie, shot out of the front gate, he looked after them and shrugged his sharp shoulders. "Guess they're pokin' into trouble. Maybe I ought to have told them about the gypsies. But it's none of my business." Then he spread his broad wings, rose above the tree-tops, and headed in the direction of his aunt's home on the Susquehanna.

XIII   *The Gypsy Camp*

"Looks more like a ditch than a canal," said Mrs. Church.

The big car had stopped on a bridge. Under it the Black River Canal ran narrow and straight and muddy. A little way north of them they could see where it ran through wooden gates to a higher level. Those were the lock gates. A boat, going up, would be pulled into the lock, the gate closed behind it; then the sluices in the upper gate would be opened. Water from above would pour in, filling the lock, and the boat would rise with the water. When it had reached the level of the water above, the upper gate would be opened, and the boat would go on. Going down, the process was reversed. These locks— of which in the Black River Canal there are in one stretch seventy in five miles—were like steps, up and down which the canal boats climbed.

"Well, no use staying here," said Mrs. Church. "He said the place was about quarter of a mile below the bridge. Can you drive down on to the towpath, Riley?"

"Yes, ma'am," said the chauffeur.

The car nosed over the bridge and turned sharp right along the towpath. It went slowly, bumping over the uneven ground. In a few minutes the canal widened out on the other side in a little bay.

"That must be the place," said Mrs. Church. "But there's nobody there now. Maybe we'd better get out and look around."

They all piled out. Alice and Emma, hot and tired from the unaccustomed jouncing, waddled down into the water. They swam across and went ashore on the other side, and pretty soon came quacking back to say that they had found a path leading back into the woods. In the meantime Adoniram had seen a boat drawn up in the bushes. He and the chauffeur got it into the water, and they all went across.

It was agreed that Freddy, as an experienced detective, who might discover clues that the others would miss, should scout up the path alone. The others sat down in the grass to wait for him, talking in low voices.

"I hope he won't run away if he sees us and thinks we're looking for him," said Adoniram. "He might, if he thinks we've come to take him back to the orphanage."

"He won't if he sees me," said Georgie. "But he may not want to go with you. He likes to live alone. You see, the people he's lived with have never been very nice."

"I think that orphanage was nice," said Freddy.

"Yes, but it wasn't on the water. Byram isn't happy unless there's a lake or a river to swim and fish in, and play around."

"Maybe this boy isn't your Byram at all," said Mrs. Church. "I don't want to be discouraging, but had you thought of that? All we've got for it, after all, is the say-so of a hawk."

"Hawks have got pretty sharp eyes," said Alice. "If he thought that boy looked like Adoniram, you may be pretty sure he does."

"Somebody coming," whispered the chauffeur.

There was a rustling of leaves and a faint leathery creaking, and a moment later a man on horseback appeared at the end of the path. He was a thin, dark man in ragged clothes, with gold earrings in his ears and a bright silk handkerchief around his neck. He stared at them a moment with sharp black eyes, then showed his white teeth in a smile and got down from his horse.

"Good afternoon, my lady," he said, bowing deeply. And as he bowed, the horse looked hard at Georgie and made a secret sign. It was a sign which every animal understands. It meant: "Don't talk. This man is not a friend to animals."

"Good afternoon," said Mrs. Church. "I hope we are not trespassing. Is this your land? We were just having a—a little picnic."

"Yes, it is my land," said the man. "As far as the eye can reach, and farther—it has always been mine, mine and my people's."

"You mean you're an Indian?"

"No, my lady. I am Romany—what you call gypsy. But you are welcome." He looked at Alice and Emma. "Ah," he said. "Ducks." And grinned at them. Alice and Emma did not like his grin: there were too many teeth in it.

Then he turned again to Mrs. Church. "But your picnic. I see nothing on the table—no bacon, no ham, no pork, no pickled pigs' feet. Where can it be?"

They all looked at one another. The remark could only mean that he had seen Freddy. But where was Freddy, then? Why hadn't he come back with him?

"We had finished," said Mrs. Church. "We were resting. As a matter of fact," she went on after a minute, "we are looking for a boy. A boy named Byram, who we understood was living in the neighborhood. Could you tell us where to find him?"

The man didn't answer. His quick eyes went from Mrs. Church to the chauffeur, to the big car across the canal, and back to Mrs. Church. "Those are very beautiful diamonds, my lady," he said. "And the pearls—like little full moons.

Is it not dangerous to wear such valuable jewels when traveling in such a wild country?"

"What has that got to do with the question I asked you?"

"Perhaps much," said the man. "Perhaps much. But your question—yes. Come back with me to my camp, let me offer you my hospitality, and I will ask my people if they have seen such a boy as you describe."

"I haven't described him yet," Mrs. Church said. "But very well, I'll come." And she got up.

"If I were you, ma'am—" began the chauffeur.

"You're not, Riley, thank goodness," said Mrs. Church. "Come along."

The gypsy went ahead, leading his horse. Adoniram carried the mice in his pocket. The two ducks brought up the rear, glancing nervously into the dark woods as they waddled along.

"I don't like this, sister," said Emma. "I don't like it at all."

"Nor do I," said Alice. "But we can't desert Mrs. Church."

Pretty soon the path opened out into a little clearing. Two wagons, like small houses set on wheels, and an old automobile with a trailer were drawn up on the far side. People were moving about, tending to the horses, cooking things over the fire in the middle of the clearing. They were dark, thin, quick-moving people, dressed in bright-colored clothes. Their queer, slanting black eyes seemed never to be looking at Adoniram, yet he knew that they didn't miss the slightest movement he made.

The gypsy led them past the fire to the other side of the clearing, and when he had spread blankets for them to sit on, he went about and talked to other members of his band in a low tone. A few bright-eyed children ran up to stare at the strangers, but an old woman drove them away. After a few minutes the gypsy came back.

"My people have not seen any boy," he said. "But if you will tell me what he looks like, we will keep an eye out for him. I think there is a chance—a very good chance—that we might be able to find him for you. Only we would expect to be paid for our trouble. We are poor people. And you are rich, my lady. I suppose you would pay—well?" And his eyes went to the string of pearls.

"I would pay a reasonable amount for any information you gave me," said Mrs. Church.

"A *reasonable* amount." The gypsy's teeth flashed in a smile. "I wonder if we would agree on what is reasonable. Those pearls, perhaps, and perhaps that diamond brooch—"

"Don't be ridiculous," said Mrs. Church sharply. "If you know where the boy is, say so, and I will pay you generously. But I certainly shall not give you my jewelry."

The gypsy's eyes narrowed. "You are unwise, my lady."

"Possibly," said Mrs. Church, getting up. "But as you do not seem to know where the boy is, I see no reason for staying longer. Come along, Riley, Adoniram."

But as they started to go, the gypsy made a gesture, and four other men slouched over from the wagons and barred their way. "This is a wild and dangerous country," said the leader, "and travelers have sometimes been known to disappear and never be heard of again. For the sake of your own safety I could not permit you to go wandering about with only this man and a boy to guard you."

"You mean that you intend to hold us here against our will?"

"Oh no, my lady. Only to guard you until it is safe for you to leave. Unless you wish to give your jewelry into my hands for safe keeping. Then it would be safe for you to go."

The chauffeur balled his fists and stepped up to the gypsy, but Mrs. Church caught him by the arm. "No, no, Riley," she said. "There are too many of them. Leave it to me." She began pulling off rings and bracelets and undoing clasps and unpinning brooches. "Very well," she said. "Turn the boy over to me and you shall have all these."

"Oh, but you mustn't do that!" said Adoniram. He didn't know much about the value of diamonds and pearls, but he knew that they were worth a great deal of money. "This is just a hold-up."

Mrs. Church smiled and shook her head at him, then she held out the double handful of glittering jewelry toward the gypsy. "Well, is it a deal?"

"Yes." The gypsy nodded to one of the men,

216

who started over toward the wagons. As they stood waiting, Adoniram felt a slight tug at his shoelace and looked down to see Eeny trying to attract his attention. He leaned down and picked up the mouse. "How'd you get down there?" he said.

Eeny ran up his arm, and perching on his shoulder close to his ear, whispered: "I sneaked away while you were sitting there and went over to talk to that horse. Listen. I found out something. They've got Freddy. They haven't decided whether to eat him or take him to town and sell him. They've got him shut up in that wagon —not the one that man's coming out of now— the one next to it. What'll we do?"

"Oh, look!" said Adoniram. Following the man, a boy came out of the wagon. He looked so much like Adoniram that, as Alice said, it made her a little dizzy for a minute. He came toward them slowly, rather unhappily. But then Georgie gave a sharp excited bark and ran forward and began jumping up and dancing about the boy, and all at once they were down in a heap on the grass, and the boy was hugging the dog

217

and the dog's tail was going like the propeller of an aeroplane.

Adoniram went over to them. "How do you do?" he said, holding out his hand. "You're Byram, I guess."

The boy got up, holding Georgie under one arm, and shook hands. "Yes, that's my name. What's yours? Have you come to take me back to the orphanage?"

"No. Georgie can tell you why we're here. My name is Adoniram. My last name is Bean now. And my middle initial is R."

Byram looked at him sharply, but before he could say anything, Mrs. Church came up. "Come along, boys. We're going back now."

The gypsies had gone back to their work, all but the leader, who was stuffing Mrs. Church's jewelry into his pockets and smiling and bowing. He seemed anxious to have them go now, and he did not follow them down the path.

As soon as they got back to the canal, Adoniram told them what Eeny had learned from the horse. "We can't leave Freddy behind," he said. "And I think we ought somehow to get Mrs.

Church's jewels back. Why, it was nothing but robbery!"

"Never mind the jewels," said Mrs. Church. "But I certainly agree about Freddy. Why, I wouldn't have anything happen to him for worlds! He's the most entertaining person I have met since I left Paris. But have any of you anything to suggest?"

So Adoniram told them about the plan he had thought of. At first Mrs. Church said it was too dangerous, but she had to admit that she couldn't think of a better one, so it was agreed that they should try it.

The chauffeur rowed Mrs. Church and the mice and the ducks across to the car and returned with Uncle Ben's alarm clock. Then he and the two boys and Georgie started back down the path to the gypsy encampment. At the edge of the clearing they put a lot of extra firecrackers in the clock, set it to begin going off in five minutes, and hid it in some bushes. Then they went on.

The gypsies were all crowded around the fire, looking at the jewelry, but when the rescue party came into sight, the leader came toward them.

"Why do you come back here?" he said angrily. "You have got what you wanted. Why do you not go?"

"Well," said the chauffeur, "you've played fair with us, so we thought we ought to warn you. There are a lot of state troopers out on the bank of the canal and I think they are coming after you."

"Let them come," said the gypsy. "We have nothing to hide." But Adoniram noticed that the others all looked fearfully toward the end of the path.

"We heard them say they were going to clean you out for good this time," said the chauffeur. "The captain said: 'No quarter, boys, remember.' They've all got their pistols out."

"I heard him say: 'Begin shooting as soon as you catch sight of them,'" put in Adoniram.

"Bah," said the gypsy. "You expect me to believe a story like that? Here you—Jeff, Adam—come back here." For two of his band were already slinking off into the woods. "Come back, I say. There isn't any—"

Bang! Bang! The first two small firecrackers went off, and the gypsies scattered and dove for the bushes. All except the leader, who stood looking uncertainly after them.

Bang! went a louder cracker, and Adoniram ducked. "Whee!" he said, "something went by my head." And at that the leader turned and ran.

The rescuers ran, too, but they ran toward the wagon where Freddy was imprisoned. As they got to the door, they could hear the crash and tramping of the gypsies' flight dying away through the woods. Adoniram had out his scout knife; in five seconds they had burst in the door, cut the ropes that bound Freddy, and as the last fusillade of giant crackers went off, they raced down the path.

A few minutes later they had rowed across the canal, got into the car, and were heading for home.

"Well," said Adoniram, "I'm glad it worked all right. But I think it's a shame about your jewelry, Mrs. Church. Can't we get the police to get it back for you?"

"Pooh," said Mrs. Church, "I told you to forget the jewelry. I can get some more at the ten-cent store."

"The ten-cent store!" exclaimed the boy.

"Of course. You didn't think those diamonds and pearls were real, did you? My goodness, no." She laughed comfortably. "You're wondering why I wear them then, aren't you? Well, they don't cost anything, and if everybody thinks they're real, what's the difference? I like 'em because they're pretty. But if nobody but a jeweler can tell the difference between a diamond costing five cents and one costing a thousand dollars— well, why spend nine hundred and ninety-nine dollars and ninety-five cents extra? It doesn't look like sense to me."

XIV *What Does R Stand For?*

Byram was grateful to his rescuers, although he said that he didn't think he would have had much trouble escaping from the gypsies, who didn't suspect how well he was able to take care of himself. They had captured him as he was fishing in the canal and had intended to keep him to work for them. The Beans welcomed him warmly, and he was grateful to them, too, for their offer of a home, but although he promised that he wouldn't run away, he had lived alone so long and seemed so unhappy in the house that finally Mr. Bean built a little cabin down in the woods, and he and Georgie moved down there.

On the first day Byram and Adoniram had a long talk. Byram agreed that they might be brothers. "But how are we going to find out?" he asked.

"Well," said Adoniram, "our middle names both begin with R, and if they are both the same, I think that would prove it pretty well, don't you?"

"Yes," said Byram. "What does your R stand for?"

"Well, I never tell anybody that," said Adoniram. "It's so silly. Why don't you tell me yours?"

"I won't do that either," said Byram.

"But if they're the same—" said Adoniram.

"You tell me yours and I'll tell you if it's the same."

"Yes, but suppose it isn't. Then I'd have told you. Now, if you'll just tell me yours, if it's different I promise I won't ever tell anybody else."

"Well, I'll promise not to tell, if you tell me yours and it's different."

"No, I can't do that."

"Neither can I."

So as neither would tell first, they didn't find out much that way.

Except on this one point, however, they agreed on everything—and indeed I suppose they agreed on this, too, if you look at it that way. They were fast friends in a week, and they fished and played and hiked together. Sometimes Adoniram stayed all night at the cabin, but Byram would never stay all night up at the house, although Mrs. Bean asked him to sometimes.

Byram was pretty suspicious of grown-ups, and I don't know that you can blame him, for, except at the orphanage, all those he had ever met had tried to shut him up and make him work for them. But after a while, when he saw that the Beans let him alone and didn't try to take advantage of him, he stopped being suspicious of them. And he would talk to them about his adventures and answer any questions they asked. But still he wouldn't live in the house, nor tell Adoniram what the R stood for.

One day a letter came for Adoniram from Dr. Murdock in Snare Forks. "I have been trying to find out where you came from and who your people were," it said, "but although I got on the track of them, I haven't much information to give you. There was a family living in the city, and during the big flood of six or seven years ago their house was carried away and they were never seen again. They had two little boys, and their names were Byram and Adoniram. But I can't find out what their last name was. It was kind of a funny name, but everybody who remembers them says it began with R."

Adoniram took the letter down to Byram's cabin and they talked a long time about it and agreed that there wasn't much doubt but that they were the two little boys.

"And if the R in our names stands for the same thing, it's certain," said Adoniram.

"If there was only some way," said Byram, "that we could find out without one of us telling the other first, we'd know."

"But there isn't."

"No, I guess there isn't."

"Well, listen," said Georgie. "I'll get the telephone book and you can show me where the names beginning with R are—because I can't read—and then I will point to all of them in turn. I'll take Adoniram first. Then if we find the name, I won't know what it is, because Adoniram will just nod his head when I point to it. Then I will go through the R's with Byram, and if he nods at the same one, we'll know they're the same. But if you nod at different ones, we'll have to think of some other way."

"Yes," said Adoniram, "but suppose some time later on you do learn to read. Then you'll know what our names are."

"I can't learn," said the dog. "I'm too dumb."

"But you might show them to somebody else and find out what they were," said Byram.

"Not if I promised not to."

So they decided to try it, and Georgie went up to the house and got the book. And he went through the R's from Rabinowitz to Ryzinski, with both of them. But their names were not there.

When they told Freddy about this, he said: "Well, how do you know your names begin with R anyway?"

Both the boys said they sounded like it.

"But has it occurred to you that they might sound like it and still not begin with R? Take the word 'gnaw,' for instance. That sounds as if it began with n, but it really begins with g."

"Do you know any names that begin with something else, but sound as if they began with R?" asked Byram.

Freddy said he didn't, but he'd bet there were some. He went back to his study and spent several hours in research. Then he came back, tired but triumphant, to announce that he had found two names: Wrench and Wrigglesworth. So then Georgie went through the names beginning with Wr, but their names were not in there either.

All the animals on the farm were interested in this search for a name, and curious to know what the boys' name really was. But there wasn't much they could do about it. Freddy spent a lot of time looking up names, and whenever he found a new one he would write it down, and then Georgie would go over the lists he made with the boys. He found a lot of silly-sounding names that began with R, such as Ratty, Rhoscomyl and Rindervieh, but none of them were right.

Of course now that Byram was found, it didn't matter so much about the name. What did matter was the reward for finding him. So many people had helped—the hawk, and Mrs. Church, and the chauffeur and the mice and the ducks and Adoniram and all the people who had written about seeing him on the canal. And then nothing had been said about what the reward was to be. The handbills had just said: "a suitable reward."

There was a good deal of talk about it in the barnyard. Some were for having Uncle Ben make medals for everybody concerned, and others felt that a cash reward would be best. Still others thought that a ticket to Mr. Boomschmidt's circus would be nice. At last it was decided to give all three. The animals still had some money left out of the bag of gold they had found on their first trip to Florida. Byram went through the letters and picked out twenty-five from people who he thought might really have seen him, and then Freddy sent two dollars and a circus ticket to each of them. Then Uncle Ben made some medals. They had an automobile on one side, with the words: "Bean-Church Expeditionary Force," and on the other, the name of the animal and the words: "Awarded for distinguished service in the Black River Campaign," and the date. A medal was given to each one who had gone on the trip to the Black River Canal, including Adoniram,

Mrs. Church, and the chauffeur, and they saved one for the hawk. So far he has never come back for it. But even though he doesn't think much of rewards, if he sees this story I hope he will stop in at the Bean farm some fall on his way south, and get it. It is a nice thing to have.

"One thing I think we really ought to do," said Freddy. "We ought to replace Mrs. Church's jewelry." So he and Adoniram went in to the ten-cent store in Centerboro and bought three dollars' worth of diamonds and pearls, and the next time Mrs. Church came to call they presented them to her. She was as pleased as anything. She put them all on and went in and had her picture taken and sent copies to everybody. Freddy had his framed and hung it up in his study beside the pictures of Abraham Lincoln and Sherlock Holmes.

The two boys had a fine time that summer. Whenever Ronald wasn't busy, they got Bertram to play with them. He was a pretty good playmate because he never got tired. The animals laughed when they saw the three of them together, they all looked so much alike.

"It tickles me every time I see 'em," said Mrs.

Wiggins. "They're nice boys, and as good as gold, all three of 'em. Even Bertram."

"He's only a rooster at heart," said Jinx.

"I suppose you mean he's chicken-hearted," said the cow. "I never did like that expression. Take Charles, now. He's no coward, except where Henrietta is concerned."

"Yes," said Jinx. "We're all cowards where she's concerned. Believe me I don't want to get her sore at me."

But Mrs. Bean was not entirely satisfied with the way things were going, and one evening at supper when the boys were picnicking at the cabin, she said to Mr. Bean: "Mr. B., I'm worried about Byram. It's all right for him to live down in the woods this summer, but what's he going to do this winter?"

"Why, I dunno, Mrs. B.," said Mr. Bean, taking a fourth helping of apple pie. "He's a good boy and can take care of himself. I can put that little stove down there for him if he wants to stay there. He could keep comfortable, seems like. Why don't you leave him be?"

" 'Tain't right," said Mrs. Bean, "and you know 'tain't right. Not when we got this big comfortable house, and nobody in it but us and Uncle Ben and Adoniram.''

Mr. Bean couldn't answer for a minute, as he had the fourth helping of pie in his mouth. But pretty soon he reached out for a fifth helping, and said: "Well, the way I look at it, Mrs. B., the boy's happy. Leave him be."

"You better leave that pie be," said Mrs. Bean, "or *you* won't be very happy." And she picked up the pie and took it into the pantry.

So Mr. Bean finished up the cheese and part of a cake and half a dozen cookies and then he went out with Uncle Ben to see if they could find a few ripe raspberries to top off with.

But the next day Mrs. Bean sent Adoniram on an errand, and she went down to the cabin to see Byram. The boy was glad to see her, for he liked and trusted Mrs. Bean, and he showed her around, and she thought everything was fine.

"You've certainly got the place fixed up nice," she said. "And Mr. Bean's going to bring down that little stove, so you'll be snug as a bug in a rug this winter."

Byram looked at her a minute, and he said:

"You—you aren't going to make me come up to the house?"

"Why, no," said Mrs. Bean. "You don't want to live in the house. And in fact I'd rather you didn't. So that's all right."

"You mean you didn't—you don't *want* me to live in the house?"

"Well, you don't want to, do you?"

"N-no," said Byram doubtfully, for it was a different thing if Mrs. Bean would rather not have him there. Always before, people had insisted on his living with them. He began to wonder if maybe it wouldn't be rather nice in the house.

"Well," said Mrs. Bean, "I just thought it was nice we both felt the same way. I don't know just why I feel that way. I like you. You're a nice boy, and I hope you'll always stay with us. But— Oh, I don't know, I suppose I feel about it just the way you do about living there. I don't know as I could tell why any better than you could. Or maybe you could?"

Byram waited to see if she meant to ask him a question, but she just sat on the old chair by the cabin door and looked off into the woods. So Byram began to think. There had always been pretty good reasons why he hadn't wanted to live in other houses. People had been unkind to him; they had made him work hard, scolded him. But as soon as he began to think why he didn't want to live in the Beans' house, he found that there weren't any reasons.

"Why," he said suddenly, "I *do* want to live there!"

"I like to hear the thrushes singing in the woods along toward evening," she said. "Like little fairy bells, I always think. Excuse me, what did you say, Byram?"

"I just said I *do* want to live in the house," repeated the boy.

"You do," said Mrs. Bean. "Well, I thought maybe you might. You see, you haven't had a very good time living with people, and so you just decided you didn't want to. I don't blame you a bit. I wouldn't either. But people are different. And I thought maybe once you began to think about it, you'd see that it might be pretty nice living in the house with Adoniram and Uncle Ben and Mr. Bean and me. We have a pretty good time. Maybe you'd have a good time too. And if you didn't,— well, you can always come back here if you want to."

So the next day Byram moved up to the house. He and Adoniram kept the little cabin to play in, and Mr. Bean put the stove in anyway, so they could use it in winter if they wanted to.

xv *Bertram, Byram and Adoniram*

There is no animal more curious than a pig, and Freddy was no exception. Perhaps that is why he was such a good detective. He just couldn't stop wondering if Adoniram and Byram were brothers, and what the R in their names stood for. Always a very sound sleeper, who snored away gently nine hours every night, it had got so that he hardly dropped off to sleep before he was broad wide awake again, wondering. And even when he dreamed, it was about names beginning with R.

To celebrate Byram's moving into the house,

the animals were giving a big party in the barn, and Freddy had to write a poem in their honor, which he was to read. But the party got nearer and nearer, and though Freddy sat hour after hour staring at his typewriter, the rhymes wouldn't come. The R key on the typewriter seemed to stand out in front of all the others. Two hours before the party was to start, all he had down was the line: "Rejoice, O animals, rejoice."

"This will never do," said Freddy. "Gosh, there must be *some* way of getting those two boys together, so they'll tell what their names are. I certainly can't write a line of poetry until I think of something. They'll just have to go without their old poem, that's all."

You can judge by this remark how upset Freddy was. For there was nothing, even his mastery of the typewriter, even his detective work, of which he was prouder than his ability to write poems.

He got up and paced the floor. "R," he said. "Begins with R. Now the letter after R must be a vowel—a, e, i, o, or u. Let me see— O-o-o-o-oh!" he said suddenly. "I've got it! I've really got it at last! Goodness, I feel quite faint."

As he sat down in the chair there was a tap on the door, and Jinx stuck his nose in. "Hi, pig," he said breezily, "how's the old muse? Steaming along a hundred miles an hour, I bet. Say, look. The guests are beginning to arrive. Hadn't you ought to be there to receive 'em? You're the chairman, or something. Oh, never mind if the old hymn of praise isn't finished. Leave off the last few lines. They'll never know the difference, and they'll be able to get to gossiping about their neighbors sooner. Poems are always too long anyway."

"Get out!" said Freddy wildly. "I'll be there, but I've got to finish. Get out!"

"O.K., genius," said Jinx, and closed the door.

Freddy wrote a few lines, then folded the paper and tucked it behind his ear. "Not much of a poem," he said, "but it'll have to do." And he went over to the barn.

It was a wonderful party, for Mrs. Church was there, and the boys, and Bertram, and even the Beans and Uncle Ben, who didn't usually come to these parties, because they felt that they made the animals too stiff and formal to have a good time. After the feasting, Freddy stood up.

"Ladies and gentlemen, friends, humans and animals," he said, "before reading to you this poem—which, I am afraid, was too hastily pre-pared, and is too short, to do adequate honor to our distinguished guests—"

"Lay off the modesty, Freddy," yelled Jinx, "and get to the work of genius."

"Well, well," said Freddy, "perhaps my rau-cous and vulgar friend is right. I will dispense with the modesty, for I have at last discovered how Adoniram and Byram can get together and find out if their names are the same. Adoniram and Byram, will you please step forward?"

The two boys came up beside Freddy. They looked at him distrustfully, but the pig said: "Don't be worried. By the method which I have thought out, nobody will ever know what those names are but yourselves, and if they are not the same, neither of you will know the other's. Now, they both begin with R. Am I right?"

"Sure," said the boys.

"Well, Adoniram, whisper the next letter in

your name to Byram."

After hesitating a moment, Adoniram did so.

"Is it the same as the second letter of yours, Byram?" asked Freddy.

Byram nodded.

"Ha!" said Freddy triumphantly. "Very well, now the third letter. The same? Fine. Now the fourth."

So they went on, and at the seventh letter they stopped.

"They're the same!" shouted Byram.

"We're brothers!" shouted Adoniram. And the two boys solemnly shook hands, while everybody cheered.

"I found out the way," said Freddy under his breath. "Won't you *please* tell me what the name is?"

But the boys smilingly shook their heads.

"Our name is Bean now," said Byram.

"Very well," said Freddy glumly. "Well, ladies and gentlemen," he shouted, waving a trotter to still the uproar, "I have written no long poem for tonight. I wish merely to offer a toast. On your feet, ladies and gentlemen."

Everybody got up.

"Bertram, Byram, and Adoniram," said
   Freddy,
"Any good farmer'd be proud to hire 'em.
   He'd never fire 'em
   Because you *can't* tire 'em.
So say we all: we all admire 'em—
Bertram, Byram, and Adoniram."

There was prolonged cheering, amidst which
the two boys, after they had bowed and shaken
hands with all the guests, led Freddy aside.

"Listen, Freddy," said Adoniram. "We've decided that we owe you such a lot, we really ought
to tell you what our name is. But you must give
your solemn promise never to tell a soul."

"Cross my heart and hope to die," said the pig
solemnly.

Then Byram bent down and whispered something in Freddy's ear.

"What!" said the pig. "It isn't possible!" And
an expression of delight spread over his face.

Then Adoniram repeated the name in his
other ear.

And at that Freddy burst out into a roar of
laughter that even Mrs. Wiggins couldn't have

equalled. He shouted and jumped up and down, the tears streaming from his eyes, and then, yelling and almost sobbing with laughter, he rushed out the barn door into the darkness. And the entire company, who had stopped talking and were staring at him, heard the sound of that enormous laughter die slowly away into the night.

And that's about all. Later, when Freddy had recovered from his laughing fit—and it took him nearly a week—Uncle Ben presented him with the diligence medal, for his persistence in studying out a way of finding out what the name beginning with R really was. But he never told anybody else, and neither did the boys. And to this day I don't know what it is myself.